AMIAYA ENTERTAINMENT LLC
Presents

Truth Hurts

by

Shalya Crape

This book is a work of fiction. Names, characters, places and incidents are either a product of the author's imagination or are used fictitiously and any resemblance to actual persons, living or dead, events, or locales is entirely coincidental.

If you purchase this book without a cover, you should be aware that this book may have been stolen property and reported as "unsold and destroyed" to the publisher. In such case neither the author nor the publisher has received any payment for this "stripped book."

ACKNOWLEDGEMENTS

I would like to first of all give thanks to God who with him all things are possible.

I can't put into words how grateful I am to Inch and Tania who allowed me the opportunity to see my dream come true and provided encouraging words along the way.

THANK YOU A MILLION TIMES OVER!

Thanks to my mother, Carole Woods, whom I give credit to for my creative abilities and my step-father (Dad as I call him) Roosevelt Woods for raising me as one of your own.

My father Bobby Crape thanks for wanting to read my short story and always keeping it real.

My kids Taysion, Kyire and Thaila, there aren't enough words that I can say to let you know mommy loves you and appreciates you not being mad at me for having to work two jobs. Remember Nothing but death can keep me from it!

Thanks to my big sisters Staci and Traci for being supportive even from a distance and giving your love throughout my life.

My sister Viva, you have been my rock since I moved to Milwaukee, thanks for staying on me and believing in me and reading all my rough drafts (smile). I can't thank you enough for helping me with the kids while busting my tail to hold down two jobs.

Thanks to my brothers Eric (I know you will read whatever I write), Tege and BJ for just being there for your little sister.

My sister-in-law, Rosa you seen me go through a lot, thanks for being there and lending a hand when you could.

My beautiful nieces Kamala and Melissa, I am so proud of you two for keeping your nose in those books and getting those diplomas. My other beautiful nieces, Megan, Kiara, Maryah, Tia, Tearah, Macayla and Samya, always remember I am here for you through it all and I love you to pieces.

My nephews EJ, Tyreen and TJ, keep your head up even though it gets harder for a black young man the older you get. My nephews Nicholas and Mackenzie, I am always your "Tee Tee" and I got your back through it all. My soon to be nephew who isn't here yet, I am waiting on your arrival and I can't wait until you get here so I can spoil you with hugs and kisses.

My best friend Michelle, you are like my sister and I love you. Thanks for listening to my ideas for the book and giving me some of your own and for being my "cheerleader".

My good friend, Deawon Delaney, thanks for just being there for me.

To my superman (you know who you are) your Diana has done it, thanks for your support

To my favorite cousin Nakia, thanks for keeping it gangsta and making sure I stayed true.

To my Gramma, thanks for all the love and the comforting words you provided and for sharing your life experiences with me.

To anyone else I missed, I love you for everything you may have done or showed me and any kind words you offered to me.

To each and every hater that doubted I was serious about this opportunity and was really pursuing it, Thank you, I feed off of your negativity.

"As long as there is air in my lungs and a beat in my heart, nothing and no one can stop me"

Shalya a.k.a. Sha

CHAPTER ONE

TRUTH HURTS

PUSH! PUSH! The nurse yelled at the young girl sitting upright in the birthing chair.

Legacy sat up and tried to breath through the pain. She was only 15 years old. Giving birth to her second baby made the doctors very concerned about her well being. The first child was a boy that she had given up for adoption since she was only 13 at the time and had been raped by her step-brother. As she continued to have contractions she thought about her life. Her drug dealing boyfriend, Trigger, was the father of her baby. To be only 16 he was known as a ruthless criminal who ruled the streets of L.A. His presence in the room was felt by everyone and even the nurses were shaken just to be around him. He sat in the chair with an unlit blunt between his fingers. Growing impatient after watching the nurses and midwives come in and out of the room he said, "Man is ya'll gone get that lil' mufucka out or what? Can't ya'll see the bitch in pain?" He continued to sit in the chair.

This would be his first baby girl and he made sure Legacy was well cared for. He had hustled hard to make sure she had everything a baby would need for the first year of its life. After finally being able to afford their own apartment he had filled the second bedroom with plenty of girl clothes, diapers, bottles and every pair of baby shoes that Footlocker would sell to him. Looking over at him and frowning at the comment he made she just closed her eyes. *How do I always end up with the wrong men?* She thought to herself. She was prepped for delivery once the nurse came in to check how many centimeters she was dilated.

"She's at 10, we need to call Dr. Armond in here." One of the nurses said.

Trigger sat up, palms sweating and heart pounding. He had never seen a baby born before and wanted to get a first hand look at his baby entering the world. Legacy began to breathe hard through all of her contractions. After several more pushes the head finally appeared along with the shoulders and the rest of the baby's body. The nurses handed the small, yellow, crying infant to her while they cleaned her off. Smiling, Legacy, knew this was her second chance at being a mother. Trigger stood up and placed the blunt to his lips while he looked at his baby girl. He watched as the tiny infant struggled to relax and get comfortable as the nurses put eye drops in her eyes and wiped her clean. Finally opening her eyes she looked at Trigger and they locked into a stare. He was lost in her eyes feeling as if he could see himself inside of her soul. Finally he told Legacy,

"We gone name her Truth." He said while rubbing her tiny head.

"Why Truth? What type of name is that for a baby?" She asked.

"Look in her eyes, baby girl is the truth fo' real."

He picked the baby up from her arms and held her looking into her eyes. The moment they shared touched Legacy's heart. She never thought Trigger would be gentle enough to handle a baby but she was seeing a different side to him. The nurses came back in the room with paperwork to fill out. While putting down her name, Legacy wrote, Truth Lashay Morrow. She looked over at the two people she loved more than anything in the world and laid back in her bed. Trigger just kept holding on to his little girl. In his mind and heart he vowed to do anything to protect her even if it took his life.

17 years later

"Truth, get in this house and finish these dishes, girl," Legacy yelled. She was tired of having to remind her daughter to do her chores. Being 32 years old, working two jobs and going to school was taking its toll on her. She wanted to move up out the hood and was trying to do all she could to stand on her own two feet. Trigger decided he was done with her since she didn't want to give him another baby and had an abortion when Truth was three years old. He never wanted to help her anymore. The only person he looked out for was his daughter. He made sure that she had any and everything she wanted at any cost. Legacy knew she had a problem on her hands when Truth was two years old and had gotten into her nail polish and decided to paint red marks all over her white couch. When she tried to discipline her, Trigger stepped in between her and looked at her with an evil, icy stare.

"Don't you fuckin' touch her Cy", he had said.

Legacy couldn't understand what the deal was with that but she came to find out later on that Trigger had a problem with anyone having control other than him. He wanted to do all the disciplining and decision making for Truth at all times.

Truth was truly a daddy's girl and everyone who knew Trigger knew not to fuck with her. Running in the house she came into the kitchen where her mother was standing.

"I don't want to do no dishes," she said folding her arms across her chest.

Legacy was getting sick of her attitude. Since she had been 13 years old she started mouthing off and testing her to see how far she would go. Trigger advised Legacy not to lay a hand on Truth or he would deal with her personally himself. Truth knew this and used it to her advantage playing both parents against each other. Sitting back against the counter she just shook her head at her daughter.

"Look you little wench, just cause ya daddy thinks he is ruling everything over here doesn't mean I have to sit up here and take this. If you continue to talk to me like that you need to get out and go live wit' him." Legacy was standing in Truth's face.

Unafraid and full of herself she stepped up closer to her mother. Both standing at the height of 5'4 they were eye to eye. Truth was her mother's miniature look alike. She was built like her and had the same creamy brown complexion. Legacy sported a short, spiked hair cut and Truth kept her hair braided up like Alicia Keys. Legacy was daring her to make a move so she could sweep the floor with her. She had grown tired of being afraid of Trigger's threats not to touch their child.

"You are such a bitch." Truth finished the last word and hit the ground.

Legacy slapped her so hard she made her fall. Looking around she reached for the phone. Legacy moved over to grab it away from her but received a blow to the back and fell right beside her daughter. Truth's eyes widened as she watched her mother jump up and grab a knife. Pointing it directly at Trigger, Legacy moved forward trying to stab him in the shoulder. Dodging her swinging arm he got behind her and held her arms behind her back putting her face down on the counter. He had walked in the door just as Truth had hit the floor.

"I told yo' ass never to touch my muthafuckin' child." He glared down at her..

"Fuck you Trigger, you don't have to be here to deal with the bullshit I do."

Legacy struggled to get free from his grip. Stepping on his toe she was able to break free and punched him in the jaw. Trigger retaliated by picking her up in one swift move and pinning her to the ground.

Scared, Truth got up and ran to her room. She heard her parent's tussling back and forth and her mother's cries and screams getting louder and louder with every blow. She packed what she could and sat on her floor with her bag until she heard silence. Fearing that her mother might be dead she didn't want to leave her room. Trigger opened her door while wiping blood from his hands and off of his rings with a towel.

"Get ya shit and let's go. Don't you call ya mother a bitch no mo' or I will do you the same way." He said

Truth quickly got up and walked out the door. Passing the kitchen doorway she noticed her mother's body crumpled up in a corner.

"Yeah, that's right, get the fuck out of here before I try to kill ya little ass." Legacy said as she picked herself up from the floor.

She saw blood everywhere from her mother getting cut by the knife she pulled.

"Get the fuck in the car," Trigger yelled.

Truth ran to the black Suburban and jumped in. The neighbors were watching from their windows. No one dared approach Trigger while he was angry. That was one of the reasons he had the nickname "Trigger," his real name was Tavarius Edwin Morrow. After his parents were killed when he was 14, he was lost to the foster system and raised on the streets. Death was the only thing he came to know so it became natural to take someone's life if they crossed him. The police never had any evidence to place any of the killings he did on him ,so he stayed out of jail only serving time for drug possession. Getting into his truck he picked up his cell phone to dial his house. One of his girlfriends, Tasty, picked up on the first ring.

"Hi bey." She said in a sexy tone.

"Look, I'm bringing my daughter home, so make the room up for her. She likes steak so fix her one and we will be there in 15." he closed his cell phone and adjusted his mirror.

Skirting off he turned up the volume on his CD player. The song *Shed So Many Tears* by Tupac, came pounding out the speakers. Truth sat back and held on to her bag afraid to speak as she watched her father light up a cigarette.

Arriving at what looked like a house on MTV CRIBS, Truth was looking around at her surroundings. She hadn't been to this house before. Trigger had so many women spread out that they each had different houses. He pulled into a gated entry way and got out as a young boy about 16 years old walked up to the car.

"Put the truck in the lower space and don't you even look at ma' baby girl or say a word to her or you'll die," he gave him a look and walked away.

Truth stared at her father as he walked away. Trigger was 6'4 with a muscular build. He was bowlegged and black in color. A very handsome man, he knew he could have any woman he wanted and he did. Sitting back in her seat she looked over at the timid boy that was now pulling the truck around to the back.

"What's your name?" she asked The boy kept silent

following orders not to even look or talk to Truth as her father directed. Truth decided to have some fun on her own.

"So you my daddy's bitch too, huh? I bet you suck his dick when he wants ya to."

That got under the boy's collar but he refused to go against Trigger knowing he was watching.

Realizing she was getting to him she went further trying to make him break every rule he was told to follow.

"I see I am gonna have ta' get really down right dirty wit ya." She smiled.

He knew she was flirting with him and he continued to ignore her as he parked the truck. Trigger wasn't one to cross when it came to Truth, his only girl. Arriving in a garage that looked like a car show room, Truth looked around and frowned. She had lived in the hood with her mother since she was five years old and hadn't seen this many cars in her life. Her daddy was living like a baller while she had watched her mother struggle to even keep a car. Getting out of the truck she saw a small red, convertible BMW with the license plates that read Baby Girl. This was the name her father affectionately referred to her as. She ran over to it and looked inside. The interior was leather with her name on the floor mats and head rests. She beamed as she ran around it. Trigger watched as she excitedly got in the car pretending to drive. He had sold a lot of weight from New York to make sure she had a car for her eighteenth birthday which was in two months.

"Hey, you ain't supposed to be in it yet, it's not August." Her father said watching her.

"Oh please daddy, please. I know this ma birthday gift, I know it. Oh my God my girls gone be jealous. Wait 'till mommy sees this." She was beaming with excitement

Trigger's face changed at the mention of her mother.

"Baby girl, you can't take this car around ya mother. If I hear you even went close to the house wit' it there will be hell to pay." Trigger didn't want the drama from Legacy that would come if she saw the car. While he didn't help her out personally he tried not to throw his success in the drug game in her face. He loved Legacy and always would but would never forgive her for aborting his son that he begged her to have.

Taking Truth inside the house he told the housekeeper, Samara, to introduce her to everyone. Surprised at the interior of the house, Truth just looked around. Jealousy began to boil in her stomach. Even though she was never without anything she felt the fact that her mother had to struggle was wrong. Tasty, the lady of the house approached her first. She was 5'7 with a very thin frame and long brown hair. Truth looked at her noticing it was a weave that she was sporting. She had to admit, Tasty was a beautiful woman and looked like a model. She was wearing a red tube top and some blue jeans with her belly ring shining.

"Hey I'm Tasty. You must be Truth cause you look just like ya daddy," she stuck her hand out.

Truth just looked at it and kept her arms folded across her chest. She didn't want to meet another woman that wasn't her mother and she made it clear she didn't like her. Two boys came walking up just as Truth was getting ready to find her father. Tasty grabbed the taller boy that looked like a young Trigger and pulled him to her.

"TJ, this here is ya sister, Truth, she is going to be staying wit' us"

TJ looked her over and shrugged his shoulders.

"I'm going to play ball. Where Trigger at?" he asked.

Truth just stared at the boy who was referred to as her brother. He looked just like her dad only shorter and without any facial hair.

14

"Damn, so we got a little sister now? That shit is crazy." The other boy said before being popped by his mother.

"I'm sorry, this is Tamaz but we call him,"

"Taz, baby, all day," he said cutting his mother off. He walked up on Truth and gave her a look over.

"Yeah, she a Morrow. All pretty and shit, gotta watch that ass now." He said.

"Boy would you watch ya language?" Tasty barked. Then she smiled at Truth.

Hurt and confused Truth wanted to run away. She always grew up with the thought that she was the only child and that she had her daddy to herself while all along he was housing a whole family on the other side of town. She began to think of her mother and wanted to call her and tell her. Reaching in her bag for her cell phone she stepped outside onto the patio right off the kitchen. Dialing her mother's number she heard her Aunt Tessa pick up.

"Truth, you need to get off your high ass horse and come see about ya momma. Cause of you she is pretty bad."

Truth immediately felt bad. Since she was used to concealing her true feelings she tried to play it hard with her aunt.

"Put her on the phone," she told her rather than asked.

"Look you little bitch, and I hope ya black ass, no good daddy, listening. I don't give a fuck who you think you is, but you ain't finna talk to me like yo' momma ain't been raising you for the last 17 years. Look around ya Truth. I bet you he took you to one of his little honeycomb hideouts introducing you to a bunch of his little crumb snatcha's. Mark my words gal, you gone learn." She hung up on her.

Truth stared at her cell phone and was angry. She threw it in the pool and walked back in. Trigger was watching her every move on camera. He had TV's installed everywhere like he was Scarface. He knew that bringing her to his home would be a change for her. Knowing she would have to grow up eventually he decided to just let it play out however it was going to be. Placing a newly rolled blunt up to his lips and taking a pull from it he inhaled the narcotic slowly as he concentrated on everything around him. Now that he was 33 he felt like his life was where it was supposed to be. He had plenty of women and more money than many people his age. Glancing at the camera that was focused on the garage he watched Truth as she walked around the new car he bought her. Trigger shook his head at the idea that one day he would have to deal with all types of drama in his life due to his daughter. She was a beautiful girl that resembled her mother almost identically. He closed his eyes and reminisced on the time he had spent with Legacy in their teenage years. While he was going down memory lane his cell phone rang. He flipped it open.

"You fucking asshole, you gon pay for taking my baby away from me. You'll see, she gon put your ass through hell, then what you gone do, call me? I should press charges on your ass for trying to beat me down when all I have tried to do is take care of what I brought into this world." Legacy was screaming into his ear.

"Look, you betta quit yellin' at me like you crazy and calm ya black ass down. She straight where she at, don't you worry. I got this now. You should be happy, I'm actually relieving ya ass of your motherly duties." He started laughing for no reason.

"Fuck you Trigger, you gone see, that's all I'm a say. You gone see the real TRUTH come out." She hung up the phone.

Trigger too high to give a care just turned up his Tupac Cd and lay back in his chair.

CHAPTER TWO

THE DRAMA UNFOLDS

The two weeks Truth had spent at her father's house were pure hell. Tasty kept trying to be overly nice by showering her with purses, clothes and shoes. Her brother TJ, who was one year older than she was, never paid her any attention and ignored her. Her other brother, Taz, was 19 and pretty much his father's right hand man. He tried to get Truth to open up but she kept to herself. Missing her friends and her mother, she wanted to go home. On the phone with her best friend, Kyisha, she released her feelings.

"Girl this house is like too perfect and so is this hoe he got here. She like, I don't know, trying too hard. Then my one brother, he ain't shit, cause he don't barely say shit to me like he got a problem wit' me being here. I just wanna go home. I can't go no where and my daddy got the place locked down like Oz and shit."

Her friend laughed.

"Girl fuck that shit then and come ova here wit' us. Boobey having a rent party in his basement Friday, you should come."

"How am I gonna get away. He got the swat team, known as my brotha's, watching my every move."

"Shit girl I don't know, tell 'em you comin' over my house and I'll come get ya," Kyisha suggested.

Truth pondered her choices for a minute while holding the line. Her other line beeped.

"Ay Ky, hol' on, my line clicked,"

She clicked over.

"Hello,"

"Hey T, how's it going over there?" It was her mother calling to check on her. She had decided to call her only child even against her sister's wishes to leave her be.

"Oh hey ma, its going good, couldn't be happier," she lied.

Legacy was hurt to hear that but she wanted Truth to be happy.

"Well I have your birthday gift for you if you want to come get it."

"My birthday isn't until August Ma!" she knew her mother knew that already.

After there was a pause Truth was the first to speak again.

"Guess what? Daddy bought me a BMW. Its red, with leather guts. Him and Tasty picked it out." She said. Truth was trying to purposely make her mother jealous.

The sound of Tasty's name produced a bad taste in Legacy's mouth. This was the same woman she had gotten arrested for beating up and slashing her tires when she was pregnant with Truth and found out Trigger had two sons by her. Trying to dismiss the fact that he was living with her, and now had their daughter living with her, she tried to remain calm and unaffected.

"Well I'm sure you'll be happy then. Did you meet your new brothers?" she asked.

Truth was surprised. She expected her mother to fly off the handle and snap but she didn't. She was even more hurt that she too knew that she had brothers and didn't tell her. Both remained silent on the phone. Truth wanted to ask if she could come home back to the normal things in life. Legacy wanted to tell her daughter she loved her and wanted her to come back home. They both sat on their pride unwilling to budge.

"Well your gift is here if you want it. I gotta go now." Legacy hung up the phone in tears.

Truth just held the line and clicked back over.

"Ky! You there?"

"Yeah, who was that?"

"Nobody,"

"Damn bitch you kept me on hold for nobody? Well next time nobody calls, why don't you hang the damn phone up? Is you coming or what? Boobey here and he wanna know." Kyisha said

"Tell him yes. I'll be there."

"He said Aight. Well look Ms. Rich and lonely I gotta go, me and Nay Nay 'bout to go to the skating rink on Crenshaw. I heard it's supposed to be jumpin' tonight," Kyisha said excitedly.

Wishing she could get away, Truth was silent for a moment as she thought about getting away.

"Well maybe I'll see you guys there," she said scheming on a plan to get there.

"Girl, how the hell you gone convince 'da gate keeper to let ya go?"

"I don't know, but I'll see ya there." She hung up and put together a plan to sneak out.

Waiting until everyone was sleep or gone, Truth crept down the spiral staircase to the lower level. Passing by the basketball court that was housed in the basement she covered the first camera with spray paint. After thinking she had all the cameras in the car garage covered she lifted the rug where she had put the keys earlier and ran over to her car. The car started up instantly with out any noise. She learned how to drive from her Uncle Day Day who had let her drive his raggedy Escort whenever he was too drunk to drive himself. Pulling out of the garage and down the driveway, she parked the car off to the side by the security gate. She jumped out of the car, running down to get her clothes that she hid behind the garbage can. Jumping back in the car she slowly drove it down the driveway and on to the street. Not knowing where she was going she stopped at a gas station. Inside the bathroom she changed into a short, red, pleated mini skirt, and a black top that had "baby-girl" on it in red letters. She fixed her weave ponytail and applied some lip gloss. Coming out of the bathroom she stuffed her clothes she had on earlier into a bag, bought a pack of gum and jumped back in her car. She flipped open her new cell phone and dialed her best friend Taysha.

"Ay T what up, where you be, I'm finna come swoop you?"

"I know this aint my uppity ass friend who moved to the south side."

"Yea it is and I'm ready to kick it. I got my own wheels now so it's on," she checked her face in the rear view. She didn't notice the black car following her.

Truth arrived in the inner city in less than 15 minutes. The night was hot and humid and everyone was out on the block. Going down Lincoln street people's heads turned at the sight of her car. Truth soaked up all the attention. Stopping in front of Taysha's house she blew the horn. Taysha jumped in and turned up the volume on the CD player. Ciara's song "OH" was playing and thumping out the bass in the speakers. Several young boys approached the car trying to holler at both girls. Across the street one of Triggers leading men Ace, saw Truth and opened his cell to call her father.

"Ay dog, yo baby girl out here trippn,' flashing and shit. What you wanna do?"

Trigger was sitting in his truck on the eastside with his boys, Burna and LJ. They were getting ready to pay a visit to some New York cat that had come into town staking out their territory. Growing angry at the news about his daughter Trigger tried to calm down.

"What she driving?"

"She got the red bitch."

Fuck! Trigger thought. He knew he had taken on too much by moving her in. Now she was gonna worry his nerves. Trying to refocus and not lose his cool he decided to let her play herself.

"Fuck it man, let her go, she'll get caught up. I'll see her on the flipside," he said calmly.

Surprised at his response Ace was unsure of how to respond.

"So just let her ride out? Man, damn, is you getting soft? It's niggas all over the car and shit."

"I said FUCK IT!" Trigger yelled. His yelling caused Burna to stop talking and turn his attention towards him.

Ace decided to drop it and shook his head. He knew that Truth had no clue as to what she was doing but he followed orders to let it go.

After hanging up Trigger called his son Taz. "Ay, yo baby sis out here in the streets. I need you to keep it gangsta' but don't be seen." He was stroking his beard, something he only did when he was nervous.

Taz knew exactly what he meant and pushed the broad up off of him that was giving him head so that he could ride off.

Truth and Taysha were cruising down the boulevard, music blasting loud when a black Neon cut her off forcing her into the other lane. Scared, she pulled over to make sure no scratches were on the car. "Girl my daddy will kill me if I scratch this car."

"Shit at least you got a car to scratch. You know some of them hoes in the hood hatn' on you cause they feel like you stuntin," Taysha was checking her makeup in the side mirror.

Truth was stunned at the comment. She didn't think she had gone that far to forget where she had come from. The black, Neon, came back around and stopped right next to her. Both girls looked at the car with its dark tinted windows. The passenger side window slowly rolled down and the faces of two young boys were seen.

"What up? Where ya'll going?" The light skinned boy asked.

Truth was mad and was not trying to talk to them.

"Ya'll nigga's almost fucked my car up and you want me to tell you where we going? Fuck ya'll bitch ass nigga's. You betta move around." Truth said.

The guys started laughing. Truth didn't know her brother Taz had sent them to get information on where she was headed to.

"Look shorty, we can tell you aint been popped yet, so why don't you let us follow ya'll and we'll get something crackin' tonite." The driver was now speaking and licking his lips while looking at her.

Truth put her car in reverse and drove off. The car followed her. Taysha was nervous.

"Girl, they gone rape us. You betta call yo daddy."

"Fuck for? My daddy is a killa,' I aint trying to get them murked. They just being men looking for new pussy. I'm gonna lead them on a wild goose chase since that's what they want." Truth said.

She drove in and out of traffic making sharp turns and

cutting down alleys. The car stayed close on her tail. Not one to give up, she was determined to lose them. Driving on the East side doing 65 down a 35 mile per hour zone, both cars were speeding down the street. Taz saw the cars fly by as he was pulling out of a McDonald's parking lot. Shaking his head he floored his red Avalanche truck to catch up to the small black car following his sister. Pulling on the side he swerved in front of the car cutting them off sending the car crashing into a parked car. Both the driver and the passenger recognized his truck and got out running. Tired of doing his father's dirty work he loaded his .35 mm and aimed it, striking both boys in the legs. Running over to them he said, "I told ya'll to follow her, not try to get her hurt. I see ya'll flying down the street and shit, what if she woulda crashed? I also made it clear if anything went wrong ya'll would pay." He held the gun to the light skinned boy's head.

Crying out in pain both of them begged and pleaded for their lives.

"Man T, come on, we were just having a lil'fun wit' her, don't kill us for dat."

"Yeah man come on, we supposed to be boys." The other one said.

Taz just shook his head again. Not a cold blooded killer like his father he decided to let them go. He picked up his cell phone to dial his father.

"Yo Trig, she got away, she too much for me, I'm going home." He told him. In the back of his mind he wished Trigger would have been more of a father to him. He raised him to be a part of the streets. Taz knew no other lifestyle except money, murder and drugs. They were more like brothers than father and son. His mother encouraged him to pursue his dreams of writing but Trigger always said, "writing is for pussy ass niggas".

Burna returned to the passenger side and they rode off. Trigger drove to the strip to find his daughter.

Truth was dancing on top of her car to the song *Bad Bitch*. She had been smoking and drinking on the strip where everyone hung out before and after the club. Taysha was drunk in the car getting her body felt on by at least two different boys.

Popping it like she knew how, Truth was shaking and rolling all over the hood of her car. People were throwing money out the window and she had drawn a crowd of men. Trigger was spotted coming down the strip by one of them. The guy tapped a few others on the shoulder and they took off towards their cars. Not noticing the crowd was starting to disperse because of her father, Truth kept right on dancing. Trigger spotted her a mile away due to the fact she had a body like her mother and she was the center of attention.

One guy was standing by Truth rubbing his hand up and down her leg while she danced. He had no clue as to who Trigger was but he was about to find out. His friend kept calling for him fearing for the worse.

"Yo Cabbie man, fuck that bitch, we gotta go, son."

"Alright man one mo minute, I might get to fuck this here tonite," Cabbie said.

Hearing what Cabbie said and angered by the entire nights events, Trigger calmly stepped out of the truck, grabbed his pistol from underneath his shirt and walked over to Truth's car. The guy, Cabbie, was drunk and still throwing money and feeling all over Truth. His friend wanted to intervene but knowing Trigger's policy of die now, talk later, he decided against it. Trigger placed the pistol to the guy's head and looked up at his drunk daughter.

"Truth, get the fuck off the car."

Lighting up a blunt he had rolled, he thought about Truth. He knew she was not cut out for the streets the way she pretended to be. If Trigger had anything to do with her upbringing she would end up being his downfall. He started his car and sped off.

Truth and Taysha sat in the car in the middle of the street breathing hard trying to calm down. They had witnessed the accident and were thankful it wasn't them.

"Girl I don't know if I should go any where but home after all this." Taysha said.

"Yeah well skating is over, its midnight and the only thing we can do is go and sit on the strip."

Truth looked at her friend and concealed her own fear. Her mother used to tell her to stop holding things in or one day it was going to affect her. They drove away and Truth's cell phone rang. It was Trigger calling. Afraid he found out she had stolen the car she tried to ignore the ringing. The phone continued to ring until she hit the silent button.

Angry that she wouldn't take his calls Trigger hit his steering wheel.

"Man, since you took in ya baby girl you been on edge. I told you them women will drive you crazy, especially when they ya own." Burna said. He had two girls himself so he could relate.

"She just so much like me its crazy. She don't give a fuck and does what the hell she wants to do." He sat there pondering his statement. He didn't want to lose his baby girl to the streets but he also didn't want to let her ruin his rep by making him soft. He lifted the girl's head that was in his lap. The trick sat up with a confused look on her face.

"Man, here take this, you slut bitch. I'm sure you got a daddy too. Go home." He handed her $20 and pushed her out of the front seat of his truck.

A drunk Truth fell after seeing her dad with a gun to someone's head right in front of her.

Her eyes were wide and she was scared.

"Daddy, don't hurt him, it's my fault I ....I'm sorry I ...just let him go and I promise to go home." Truth was afraid. Feeling guilty she wanted to do all she could to save the innocent man.

Once Trigger was angry there was no limit to the release of his self control.

"Do you think I give a fuck about this yuppie ass nigga right here? Do you? He ain't shit but here he stands putting his muthafucking hands on my baby girl." Turning to face Cabbie he said, "No one touches my baby girl," He pulled the trigger *"Bloom!"* and shot him in the head.

His body dropped to the ground with blood pouring out. His friend just shook his head as he watched his homey get murdered. Helpless, he drove off with tears in his eyes.

Truth was screaming and Taysha had run off down the street. Burna, used to cleaning up all of Triggers outrageous actions, dragged the body of the boy he had shot and shot it again making sure he was dead. Taking the pistol away from Trigger to make sure he didn't do anything to hurt his own he got back into the truck and waited. Sirens were heard in the distance. Trigger immediately jumped back in his truck and yelled at Truth,

"Yo, get that car home or else." He quickly sped off.

Truth nervously jumped in her car and drove away from the scene passing by several cop cars and ambulances on their way. She knew she shouldn't have crossed her father like that. Her mother warned her for years not to ever cross her father or make him angry. She was afraid to go home. Trigger was sitting in his Cadillac Seville after telling Burna to take the truck and park it for awhile until the death of the boy he killed passed over. He thought about everything he had done in his life and actually was remorseful for two seconds. He didn't mean to kill the boy like that in front of his daughter but he was a man of his word. He knew he should have handled the situation better but all he knew how to do was kill. He lit up a blunt and took a long drag from it. He rubbed his goatee and looked out the window. *She gone be the death of me* he thought and drove away to his apartment to be alone away from everyone.

Truth parked the car in front of the big house and stared at it. She was not going to live like that forever. Tears were rolling down her face because of the boy she had gotten killed. Her father was too protective of her. She decided she was going to show him that she didn't need him like he thought. Her mother crossed her mind again. Wiping away the tears, she drove into the parking garage and locked the car up. She decided to step up her own little plan to get away. She was determined to show them that she was a survivor. Only she wasn't prepared for what was going to happen in the years to come.

CHAPTER THREE

I CAN DO BAD BY MYSELF!

Truth packed all of her clothes and emptied her piggy bank that contained $1500 she had been saving for school clothes. Trying to get away before her father or anyone else noticed she packed the car up and drove to the West side to her friend, Laquetta's house.

Laquetta was four years older than Truth. They had become friends when Truth was 8 years old and had to stay with them when her mother was arrested for battery against one of her father's girlfriends. Living in her own apartment with her 25 year old boyfriend Dame, Laquetta was no stranger to struggle. She was jealous of Truth deep down but never showed it. Truth had asked if she could stay with her until she figured things out.

"Come on in T, girl you know you welcomed here," Laquetta said.

She noticed the brand new BMW parked out front and turned her nose up. She didn't like the fact that Truth was spoiled but she refused to let her know it.

"Thanks La La. Girl, my daddy and my momma think they

can rule me, but I'm finna be 18 in a few months and a bitch is tired of dealing wit' they drama," Truth set her bags down and looked around the small apartment. It was cute but very tiny with minimal decorations.

"Yeah but you gon have to pull ya own weight cause I got my own problems and can't take on yours. So you can kick in on the rent, about $200 a month." Laquetta was using it to her advantage. With her having a baby and being on rent assistance her rent was only $50 a month.

Truth was ok with the amount and figured she would only need to crash a couple of months before she moved around.

Once Trigger found out Truth moved he called Legacy to locate her whereabouts.

"Cy, I know we ain't been on the best of shit, but Truth is gone and I need to locate her ASAP. What do you know?"

Legacy was sitting at her kitchen table smoking a cigarette and drinking her third cup of gin and orange juice. She had picked up a drinking habit ever since Trigger took Truth away from her.

"You know what Trigger, I don't even give a fuck where that bitch is. Ya'll two are just alike and I'm glad she is now your problem. So deal wit' it muthafucka," she hung up.

Trigger's anger escalated. He was going to deal with both Truth and Legacy. His hustling had started to slip and he wasn't bringing in as much money as he was before. He decided to leave Truth wherever she was and take a vacation to the Bahamas with one of his girls, Nikkie, a slim Puerto Rican, who gave the best head. He would handle her when he got back.

After staying with Laquetta for two weeks, Truth began to notice her jealousy. Every now and then she would over hear her and Dame arguing. Today when she arrived home from school she walked in to another one of their brawls.

"That little bitch is getting on my fucking nerves acting like she the finest thing on the West Coast. She gon get her head cracked one day" Laquetta said.

"You just mad cause that girl still pulling niggas from every which a way and you got a baby." Dame said. He was not the father of her one year old son, Isaiah, but he helped her when he could.

Angered by what he said, Laquetta snapped. "You probably wanna fuck her don't you? I see how you watch her. If you even so much as try to get near her I will call your P.O. on you and report to them all the shit you out here selling on the corna."

"You insecure La. That girl ain't tryna upstage you. Betta watch it for you cross her and she turn in to her crazy ass daddy." He said.

Truth just shook her head, hurt that her friend thought of her like that. She decided it was time to make moves again. That night while she was asleep she felt a hand on her thigh. Thinking she had been dreaming she ignored it until the hand moved to her breasts.

She opened her eyes only to see Dame in his boxers standing over her. Her eyes widened at the sight of him with no shirt on. He moved her sheet aside and stared at her body. Truth just lied there in the bed. In her mind she knew she should have stopped him but she was attracted to him in a way she never knew. He had been flirting with her off and on and had finally made his move. She sat up in the bed and they stared at each other. Lifting up her t-shirt she let him do what he wanted. He climbed on top of her and fondled her body. Being a virgin she was nervous but very aroused by his touch. After kissing her he pulled his boxers down. Truth was scared at the sight of his penis. She held her breath as he tried to penetrate her. After about five minutes of trying to break past her opening he finally was able to get in. Taking her virginity he used her body for his pleasure. Once he finished, he got up and went into the other room to lay down with a sleeping Laquetta who had no idea what Dame had just done. Feeling guilty for letting her friend's man have his way with her, Truth knew she had to leave before Laquetta found out.

She packed her stuff and left $200 on the bed to help cover the rent and hit the streets. Most of her friends lived with their parents or were in worse situations than she was so she knew she couldn't run to them. She couldn't go home to her mother or Legacy would tell her father. Cruising the streets alone with no where to go she pulled into a motel parking lot. With only $500 left to her name she rented a room with her fake ID that said she was 21. Walking to her room she passed by a group of guys. All of their heads turned as she walked by. One of them decided to try his luck with her.

"Say mami, what's a girl like you doing at a place like this? You getting down?" he asked.

Truth continued to walk.

"Damn you not gon speak to a nigga? What's up, you too good?" the other one said.

"Man, leave that stuck up hoe alone and come on," one of his friends said.

Not one to give up he caught up to her and grabbed her arm.

Truth swung at him hitting him in the jaw. "Don't you ever fucking grab me like that. You don't know me," She said defensively.

Holding on to his face homeboy wanted to retaliate but he would never hit a girl.

"Damn you got a hell of a punch." He spit blood out.

Dude's friends were laughing at him.

Embarrassed, he decided to leave Truth alone. Truth felt bad that she had hit him.

So she said, "I'm sorry, it's just that I don't take to men touching me aggressively."

He looked at her and shook his head.

"My name is Truth and yours?" She stuck her hand out.

"It's Tommy but they call me T-bone." He shook her hand and continued rubbing his jaw.

She looked him over completely for the first time. He had to be about 5'11 and 195 pounds. He had on an orange and white plaid button up shirt and baggy blue jeans.

Around his neck was a heavy platinum chain with a cross hanging from it. In his ears were diamond studs. Truth liked what she saw standing before her.

"Well Tommy, maybe I'll see you around." That was her way of making men come after her.

Tommy just looked at her and smiled. He knew she wanted him to pursue her so he just played her at her own game.

"Alright Truth, stay up." And he walked away

Shocked, her mouth fell open. Never had anyone walked away from her without sweating her for her number. Not one to be outdone she decided to be bold. "Uh, Tommy, I'm saying, can I get ya numba' and maybe we can just be cool? You have to at least let me make it up to you for socking you in the jaw." He smiled and turned back around to give her his number.

After talking to him on the phone Truth learned that T-Bone was 21 and was originally from New York. He moved to the West Coast and was living in his own apartment near her mother on the West side of Los Angeles. T-Bone told Truth that he didn't have any kids and worked construction to cover the fact that he was a hustler. After returning to her hotel room Truth thought about what she was going to do to take care of her self. She decided she was going to keep Tommy as close as possible until she could figure something out.

Trigger combed the streets day and night looking for Truth. After she had been gone for two weeks he decided she was basically telling him to fuck off. None of her friends had seen her and she had skipped school. Trigger was going to teach Truth a lesson about trying to grow up so fast. He put a trace out on her car. Opening his cell phone he called one of his friends.

"This Loc," the guy answered.

"Ay, 'member that lil' red number I bought from Dip? I need to find it." Trigger lit a cigarette and waited.

Loc put him on hold and called up "Dip," a car salesman in San Francisco.

"D, this Loc. My man looking for that red Beamer he bought, can you trace it for me?"

"Sure no prob, give me twenty and I'll hit ya back."

Loc clicked over to Trigger. "We'll have it in 20,"

"Alright. One!" Trigger hung up and wished he had been a better father to Truth. She was spoiled and didn't want to have anything to do with him since she found out about his other kids. His cell phone rang as he sat on his bike deep in thought. Looking at the caller ID it was Burna.

"Trig, we found it in San Fernando at some motel. She seems to be alone but I did notice a nigga wit' her. She don't look like she suffering none."

"Who she wit'?" he asked

"Some cat from New York, he holdin' too, big money. Pushing a 'Lac truck on Dub Two's."

Trigger took in all the info he received. He hated cats from

New York. They were too flashy and he always had beef with them. Now his daughter was caught up with one.

"Take it. The spare is in the gas cap." He instructed. Starting his bike, he sped off doing a wheelie to burn off his frustration.

Truth sat in her hotel room talking to Tommy. Over the past two weeks the two became inseparable. He would take her everywhere with him. She had lied and told him she was 19. He was intrigued by her because she carried herself much older than some 21 year old women. Sex hadn't come up yet because Tommy never pushed the issue. He figured she was a virgin because she never tried him like most women did.

Looking out the window he noticed a man fiddling with the gas cap on her car.

"Truth, someone is messing wit' yo car,"

Truth jumped up and ran to the window. She noticed a man taking a key from her gas cap and getting in her car.

"What...how ......?"

She didn't know where the guy came from. By the time she had time to think Tommy was out the door and running. He pulled a Beretta from his waist and ran up to her car.

Pointing the gun at Burna's head he spoke slowly and calmly.

"Get the fuck out the car and no one will get hurt."

Burna tensed up and knew if he went for his gun it would be trouble.

"Look lil' dude. You don't want to fuck wit' this here. Just let me take the car and I'll be out ya way."

"Naw muthafucka! I don't know you,son ! Just get out my girls ride and we cool," He cocked his hammer.

Burna tried to think fast. He saw Truth coming up to the car.

"Tommy be cool, please, it's just a car. Let's see why he tryna take it," Truth didn't want to witness another murder.

Tommy pulled back waiting on his answer. He and Burna never unlocked eyes.

"Truth, tell ya man here that Trig aint one to be crossed." Burna was pleading with her. At the mention of her father Truth stepped back and looked at Burna. She had no idea how her father seemed to always be one step ahead of her by sending his henchmen to do his dirty work. Deciding that she had enough, Truth grabbed Tommy by the arm.

"Let him take it. It's just a car. Please, I don't want to cross my father," she pleaded.

Tommy didn't want to let up but he did. He put his Beretta back in his pants and gave Burna a look. He walked over by his truck to calm down.

Truth stared at Burna. "Whateva it is that Trigger has you doing to check up on me tell him I got this." She said and walked away.

Burna started the car and drove off shaking his head. He knew Trigger wouldn't like hearing that. Always one to be in control of everything Trigger couldn't handle someone saying they didn't need him.

Truth and Tommy got into his truck and he took her out to breakfast. He wanted to ask more about her father but decided to stay away from the subject for the moment. After the couple ate he surprised her by taking her to the car lot. He purchased a used, black, convertible, Sebring for her. While he had money, he didn't have the type of money, Trigger had to buy a $50,000 vehicle. Elated, Truth was jumping up and down. She thanked him over and over.

Over the course of the next month Tommy stayed by Truth's side helping her out by giving her money and making sure she had everything she needed. He let her move into his apartment in the inner city. He continued to travel back and forth from coast to coast making sure he stayed in contact with his connects. One day while he was away on one of his trips, Truth was at home alone. Walking around in her silk robe she felt a sudden wave of nausea sweep over her. Truth ran to the bathroom to return her breakfast in to the toilet. She wiped her forehead and looked at her face in the mirror. She realized she was picking up weight but figured it was due to stress. She wanted so bad to call her mother to check on her and tell her she was ok but she decided not to. She never thought about how much trouble she was causing by not going to school and lying to Tommy about her age. Her father had backed off ever since he had taken her car away.

Walking to her closet to find something to wear, she heard a knock at the door. She ran to the door, looked out the window and found her friend Taysha standing at the door.

"Oh my God girl, where you been?" Taysha asked when she opened the door.

Truth was happy to see her. Since she had been with Tommy she had gotten caught up and forgot about her friends.

"Girl, I been chillin,' what up?" Truth said

"Damn you been chillin' alright, you done got all thick and shit, so who is he?"

Truth was about to tell her about Tommy when her cell phone started ringing. The caller ID showed Laquetta's number. Not sure as to why she was calling she picked up the call.

"Hello," Truth answered.

"Look you lil' bitch, I knew you was no good. How you gon go and fuck my man,

you was supposed to be my friend. You betta' watch ya back. You burnt him and he turned around and burnt me. I knew it was you. I just knew it. You hoe. You gon get yours." Laquetta screamed at her.

Confused, Truth thought about the incident a month prior with Dame and tried to fix it.

"I.... well he came on to me and I couldn't of burnt him because I never been with no one else."

"Yea whateva, you trifling ass hoe. Don't let me catch you in the streets." Laquetta said and hung up.

Taysha caught the tail end of the conversation. "Damn ma, you fucked Quetta's man? Girl you betta hide, you know that bitch crazy. That's why her baby daddy left her cause she tried to kill him."

"I am not worried about Quetta at all ,but I do need to get to a doctor. She said he burnt her and I'm wondering if he burnt me too. Do you know any free clinics?" she asked.

Truth and Taysha hopped in her car to go to the free clinic located downtown. On the way there Taysha tried to tell Truth about her mother.

"You know Truth, you really need to check on ya mom's. My Aunt Muffin said she ain't doing too well. She drinking real heavy and got fired from her job." She stopped to check for her expression but Truth kept a stone face.

Truth was hurt to hear that, but didn't let it show. She still didn't want to convey her feelings. "That's too bad, do I turn here?" she asked

Taysha shook her head at her friend. She knew she would learn one day.

At the clinic the doctor checked her in and asked how many partners she had been with. Recalling the one time with Dame she listed just one. The doctor checked her out for all venereal diseases and found she had contracted Gonorrhea which would explain why she had pain when she used the bathroom. She was glad she hadn't slept with Tommy even after a month so that she didn't pass it on to him. Truth walked back in the room where the doctor was sitting and asked for her prescription for penicillin. The doctor asked Truth when did she get her last period and Truth couldn't remember. She had been so preoccupied that she hadn't noticed that she skipped it.

"Honey, we got your urine test back and you tested positive. You're pregnant" the doctor said. She looked at her with concern feeling that Truth was another young girl who had gotten caught up.

Truth's heart stopped and she couldn't breath. *PREGNANT!* She thought she didn't know what to do. There was no way she could raise a baby alone. She got up off of the table and watched while the doctor gave her information on abortion clinics and adoption resources. She knew it was Dame's baby because she hadn't been with anyone else. She walked out into the waiting room in a zombie like state which caused Taysha to jump up and run to her.

"Truth, you are scaring me, what's wrong? What did they say?" she asked as she helped Truth out to the car.

"I'm four weeks pregnant." That word felt like a ton of bricks. She knew she couldn't tell Dame about it since Laquetta was already looking for a reason to fight.

She didn't even know if she wanted to keep it. She was only 17 years old and only 2 weeks from being 18. She let Taysha drive her car. It was a times like that she needed her mother. She sat back in the passenger seat and for the first time she let the tears roll down her face in front of her friend.

On the other side of town dressed in an Armani business suit, Trigger sat discussing business with a group of men. He had just made a new connect with a Latino, named Ricos. He offered a better deal for 50 kilos than Trigger's old connect so he decided to take it. After the meeting was over Trigger was happy because his business had slipped over the course of a month. His cell phone vibrated in his pocket. Walking out the door to his truck he flipped it open.

"Yo this Trig, what up?"

"Well I see some people never change." It was one of his old flames, a chick named, Tarina.

A smile spread across his face. Tarina was a beautiful girl, a mix of black and Asian. Trigger used to mess with Tarina back when he was in high school at the same time that he and Legacy were dating. Tarina never wanted to be with Trigger after high school. She went on to college to study to be a doctor and ended up marrying a high profile lawyer. Wondering why after so many years that she was calling, Trigger was definitely curious.

"So Ms. Ree Ree, why are you on my phone?"

"It's Mrs. now and I don't go by Ree Ree anymore. Just call me Tarina." She paused for a moment.

Trigger was still confused as to how homegirl got his number and why she was on his phone. Tarina knew what type of guy Trigger was and was glad she hadn't gotten involved with him except for the sexual encounter in high school.

"Look, I really am not supposed to do this but I had a feeling that you didn't know, and, well, that you might could help." She said

Trigger was sitting in his truck waiting on her to continue.

"You know I am a doctor now and I work at the free clinic downtown on my light days. Well I know seventeen years ago you and Legacy Marshall had a baby girl, and today in my office I seen a girl by the name of, Truth Morrow. I knew she had to be yours cause she has those eyes and that attitude she carries is just like you. Anyhow, I could lose my license to practice if you tell anyone I told you this, but she is pregnant."

She paused to let it sink in.

Trigger's heart jumped out of his chest. He was hurt and upset but neither emotion did he reveal on the phone.

"So why are you telling me?" He asked

Knowing he would say that she had already prepared for him to act uncaring.

"Trigger I know I am not apart of that lifestyle, but you know I grew up in the hood and since my mother refuses to move out of that neighborhood I still hear things. Lil' Davey tells me stuff."

Lil' Davey was her nineteen year old brother who was still living at home with their mother.

Trigger rubbed his goatee.

She continued. "Lil' Davey said it was some girl named Truth that had messed around with her friend's man and now the girl is looking to do her harm. He is friends with the guy she messed with and he was saying it's messed up how far this other girl is going to try and hurt her. I was concerned after I seen Truth in person and realized she was your daughter. She looked so distraught, Trigger. I knew she wouldn't let me in cause she is so much like you in her personality, it's like I saw you in a female form. All I am saying is she needs one of her parents right now and I know how you feel about her."

Trigger sat holding the phone trying to collect his thoughts together on the information he just heard. Part of him wanted to kill whoever had gotten Truth pregnant and the other part wanted to kill Truth for getting pregnant. He was for once in his life, speechless.

"Thanks Tarina for looking out. I'll see if I can talk to her." He wanted to end the conversation before his anger erupted again.

"Trigger, please do it for her. I see so many young girls go through life alone and make the wrong decisions. You can save your baby girl if anybody can. Think about how you and Legacy were at 15. I know you don't want Truth to be with someone like you." She knew her last comment hit him hard.

He almost dropped his phone after feeling like someone punched him. Tarina was the only woman he would ever have allowed to say something like that to him. They grew up together and were friends even before they had gotten involved sexually.

Hanging up Trigger felt like someone was sitting on his chest. He didn't know how to handle the situation without someone getting hurt. He tried to reach out to Legacy to see if she would be more cooperative knowing her daughter was pregnant. He called her on the phone but was unable to reach her. He drove his truck to the West side of town to see if she was home. He arrived at her house fifteen minutes later and walked up to her porch. He found it strange that Legacy's front door was wide open and she wasn't answering the phone. Walking in, the place smelled like the garbage hadn't been taken out in days. There were empty soda cans and dishes piled up in the sink. Trigger found it to be unusual for Legacy because she was a pretty clean person.

"Cy- Cy!" he called. It was the nickname he had given her. There was still no answer.

Trigger walked upstairs to the bedrooms and passed Truth's old room which was exactly the way she left it. Reaching the master bedroom the door was closed and there was music playing. He tapped on the door and received no response. Opening the door Trigger almost fainted from the sight of his baby momma performing oral sex on his best friend, Burna. "What the fuck, man?" he asked angered

Legacy jumped up and covered herself. She looked a mess.

Her hair was matted and she hadn't cleaned her bedroom. There were clothes everywhere and the smell of incense and crack filled the air.

"Fuck you doin' here?" she asked.

She refused to look him in the eye fearing he would see all the hurt and pain she was experiencing. Burna just stepped aside after zipping up his pants and collecting his money for the "eight ball" he had just sold her. Trying not to make eye contact with Trigger he stepped around him and went out the door. Trigger wasn't mad about the fact his friend was getting head from his baby momma ,but more so that she was now a crack head getting served by his best friend.

"Damn Cy, what happened to you, ma?" he sat down on the bed next to her and rubbed her hair.

Ducking away from him she was ashamed. "*You* happened to me, that's what." She tried to cover her naked body with her worn and tattered robe.

He stared at her and almost shed a tear but his pride allowed him to mask his true feelings. He felt terrible that he may have had something to do with her picking up a bad

habit and completely losing herself. He rubbed her cheek with his hand remembering when they were only 16 and Truth was a year old.

"Do you remember when your momma wouldn't let us stay with her cause Truth cried too much? And how we had to eat peanut butter and jelly sandwiches and stay wit' my Uncle Dank in his one bedroom apartment?" he looked into her big, brown eyes.

She looked down at the floor. Her eyes were filling up with tears. She missed her daughter very much and was feeling sorry for herself.

Shaking her head she put her hands on her face covering her

eyes.

"I miss ma baby Trig. She was all I had." The tears were falling from her eyes. He grabbed her hand and swallowed down his emotions as he prepared to tell her about the pregnancy.

"Cy, it's somethin' I gotta tell ya so ....here goes." He couldn't believe how difficult it was dealing with the fact his baby girl was pregnant.

"Ya baby. Our baby girl, is finna be a momma." He again choked down his anger at the thought of Truth with a big belly. Legacy frowned and stared at him. Her eyes widened in amazement. She couldn't believe what she had just heard him say. Her heart broke in two pieces and she couldn't do nothing but blame herself.

"Lord, not her. Not Truth, she supposed to be everything I wasn't," She sobbed into Trigger's arms. He held her and buried his face in her hair releasing a tear of his own. He truly, for the first time, felt defeated. Sitting back up Legacy assumed a role that was taken away from her for almost 2 months.

"Look Trigger, she only 17, she can't handle no baby alone. I don't care how stubborn she is and how much she is like you, she needs both of us right now." She looked up at him making eye contact for the first time. They both sat staring at each other. Trigger was caught off guard at all the feelings and emotions he had felt for Legacy as they came back to him. Through all of the women he had been with he knew

Legacy was his first real love. He couldn't explain it but he still loved her and always would.

"Well ....I ...I don't know where she is." He stumbled through his words

"What you mean. You mean ma baby is pregnant and alone?" Legacy got up and started pacing the floor. She caught sight of the crack pipe lying on her dresser. Staring at it for a long time she knew she had to pull it together.

Trigger got up from the bed, went in his pocket and pulled out $500. He walked over to Legacy and slipped it in her hand.

"Get it together ma. You betta than this shit here." He picked up the pipe and broke it in half. He walked out of the room and went downstairs to get into his truck.

Truth was back at the apartment she shared with Tommy trying to figure out what to do. She paced back and forth deciding on whether or not to have an abortion or keep it. She knew she could ask Tommy for the money but she didn't want to let him know she was pregnant. Sitting down at the table she thought of a plan.

• • •

Later on that week when Tommy returned home he was greeted by a half dressed Truth wearing a red silk, see through teddy. He was instantly aroused. They hadn't had sex because he stayed gone so much and he didn't want to rush her into anything. He had fallen in love with Truth and didn't want to be too forceful. She handed him a glass of wine and she walked over to him in her red pumps with the 2" heel.

"Hey, welcome home," she smiled

To be only seventeen years old Truth had a body of a grown woman. Her breasts were spilling out of the top of the teddy so every time she moved her chest jiggled. She bent over in front of him revealing the matching thong she had on. He wanted to take her right there in the living room but he waited patiently to see what she had in store. Truth had ordered Chinese food and had the food all spread out on the table. After a quiet candlelight dinner she decided to seduce her man. Walking over to the stereo, she turned on the CD player and

Marques Houston's song Naked came on. She started rolling her hips and turning around in circles like she was on a stage working for money.

Tommy sat back licking his lips taking in everything that was happening. Once the song ended she had climbed on his lap and started kissing him. He picked her up and carried her to the bedroom where she had rose petals all over the bed and the floor. Slowly, Tommy slid the teddy down her body kissing everything that was revealed as he inched the fabric down. When Truth was fully naked, he slipped his shirt off revealing his six pack and a tattoo on his stomach that read *Only God Can Judge Me*. Truth rubbed her hands across the letters painted on his stomach, grabbed his face and kissed him long and hard. He planted kisses along her thigh before sliding his tongue over her swollen clit. Tommy kissed and sucked until Truth was grabbing at his head. She had never experienced an orgasm before and was floating on cloud 90. She held on as he took her back and forth over and over until she had his face glazed over. Penetrating her he thought would be difficult but it wasn't. Her vagina was tight and wet but he could tell she had already lost her virginity which he was glad of because he would feel guilty to take it away. Once he found a rhythm they both held on to each other lost in the pleasure of the moment. Truth was crying because she had never experienced love before and it felt so good to her. When Tommy tried to pull out so that he wouldn't ejaculate his seed inside of her Truth wouldn't let him. She held on tight and he had no choice but to release himself within her. They lay in each others arms and Truth had a smile on her face because her plan had worked. After hearing his phone vibrate on the nightstand, Tommy woke up to answer it.

"Yeah," he said

On the other end was the voice of a female. "I know you laid up wit' that bitch while I'm here pregnant wit' ya baby. I guarantee you she gone be ya downfall."

Sighing, Tommy just shook his head. He didn't want to deal with his wife, Tiffany's drama and sure hadn't told Truth about her.

"Look, a nigga sleep, so gon wit that bullshit."

"Well you gon be sleep a long time nigga cause I got a feeling about ya ass and that bitch you fucking, she bad luck. It's just a matter of time before what I say comes true."

Tommy was tired of dealing with Tiffany's premonitions. She had told him years before that she was psychic and was able to see into the future but nothing she ever saw came true.

"Whateva," he hung up the phone and turned back over to put his hands around Truth.

Truth was awake and heard Tommy's end of the conversation. Being naïve and in love she dismissed all the questions burning in her head about who was on the other end of the phone and went back to sleep. She figured she would let it die and come back to it later. Her plan to make Tommy her baby daddy was going to take place, this she was sure of. Rolling over she placed her arm around him and kissed him on the cheek. She breathed a sigh of relief and moved her hand across her stomach feeling nothing at all but envisioning her life as a mother. Tommy moved toward her and put his hand across hers. Whispering to her he said,

"Truth, I love you."

He kissed her on her forehead. She smiled knowing everything would be ok.

CHAPTER FOUR

REVENGE IS A BITCH!

Two weeks later!

While lying in the bed on her eighteenth birthday, Truth awoke to breakfast in bed. Tommy came in carrying a tray filled with waffles, eggs, bacon, orange juice and a dozen roses with a diamond tennis bracelet around them. Elated, she sat up and instantly became dizzy. Feeling nauseated she got up and ran to the bathroom. Deciding now was a good time to break the news she came back into the room and sat down on the bed. Tommy helped her put on the bracelet and kissed her on the forehead.

"Uh T? I gotta tell you something. I'm not sure how you gone take it but..."

He cut her off, "You pregnant, aint you?" he smiled.

She looked up at him and tears came to her eyes. Her conscience told her she was wrong for what she was doing. She ignored that part and continued on in her charade. She was about six weeks pregnant and was going to make Tommy think she was only two weeks.

"Yeah I am. I can't keep nothing down and I know I need to

get to a doctor to handle it cause I know you on the grind and everything and well, I'm too young for a baby and I know you aint trying to…" he shushed her.

"Truth, I can handle it. This baby is going to be born and we are going to make sure he or she will have the best of everything. Don't worry boo, I got you." He kissed her lips.

He took her shopping on Rodeo Drive and let her get a few items for herself and the baby to be. Afterwards he took her to trade in her Convertible Sebring for a brand new Ford Explorer. He told her the baby would need to ride in comfort and since he had been moving more weight with his new connect back home in New York, he was bringing in more money. This was causing beef with the niggas on the streets of L.A. who were accustomed to having it all locked down. One person in particular had taken notice to this new cat. Trigger scratched at his freshly lined goatee as he listened to LJ tell him about Tommy.

"Yo dog, lil' man is holding heavy. If we can connect with him we can take over what he has, do away wit' him, and be the rulers in this here city."

"I told you man, I don't like this nigga, it's something you mentioned about him that sounds familiar to me." Trigger tried to figure out how he knew about Tommy. He dismissed the thoughts of remembering him and put into a plan of action to take him down.

•   •   •

After getting herself clean from the drugs and alcohol she had become addicted too, Legacy was looking like her old self again. Her hair had grown out and her complexion had returned to its smooth texture. She was released from the treatment program after 8 weeks. Wanting to find her daughter,

Legacy cleaned up her house and built up her nerve to call her cell phone.

"Yeah," Truth answered on the first ring not recognizing the number.

"Uh... hey there, Truth! This is ya momma!"

Truth was sitting in a McDonald's drive thru with Taysha and Aneedra, her friend from school. Speechless, she didn't know what to say. She hadn't talked to her mother since she had moved in with Tommy. "Hey ma," was all she could say.

They both held the line.

"You ok? Do you need anything? I just wanna tell you ....I am here ...when you need me...and I ......love you!" Legacy relaxed, happy she was able to get that out.

Truth's emotions started coming out more now that she was pregnant.

She decided to be upfront and real with her mother and tell her she was pregnant. As she started to tell her, a car smacked into the back of her brand new truck.

"Ma, I gotta call you back," she said and hung up the line. Laquetta had slammed her Ford Taurus into the back of the truck and was trying to do it again. Backing up and stepping on the pedal she lunged forward knocking the trunk inwards. The girls screamed.

"Truth, I told you that bitch was crazy, now she tryna kill us," yelled Taysha.

Truth pulled over and Laquetta followed. Jumping out she ran to Truth's side and grabbed a hold of her hair through the window, slamming Truth up against the steering wheel. Taysha jumped out and ran around to pull Laquetta off, only to be jumped by two other girls who Laquetta had brought with her. In the truck Truth was at an unfair advantage because she was still in her seat belt and couldn't move much but to swing at

Laquetta. Aneedra undid her seat belt for her and jumped out to help Taysha who was pinned down.

"Truth this yo shit, handle that bitch, NOW!" Aneedra yelled.

Truth opened the door with her strength pushing Laquetta down to the ground. Once she was down she jumped up on her and it turned into a girl fight. Passer bys and people from McDonald's stopped and stared but no one dared to break it up. Laquetta punched Truth in her stomach knocking the wind out of her. Gathering her self together Truth pulled herself up and more blows were received and given out. Both girls had each other by the hair and were swinging their arms. Laquetta broke free and went for her purse.

"This bitch finna die," she yelled

Aneedra and Taysha wrestled the girls off of them and watched as Laquetta pulled her small .22 out and was about to open fire on Truth, when she was struck in the shoulder by TJ, Truth's brother. He had been sitting in his car with his girlfriend, Shaquena, when he seen the gun Laquetta pulled out. Trying to protect his only sister, he had pulled the pistol he kept in the car taped under the seat, aiming for the girl. Laquetta fell to the ground in pain. Her friend Tawana grabbed the .22 from her hand and fired it.

Truth screamed as more gunfire erupted and she was hit in the chest. Everyone scrambled for cover as they watched bodies dropping to the ground to avoid stray bullets. Aneedra, Taysha and TJ ran over to where Truth lay bleeding.

"Stay with us Truth, please. Oh God, please call an ambulance," yelled Aneedra.

After 10 minutes, police arrived at the scene along with two ambulances. TJ had already fled the scene and called his brother Taz in a nervous panic.

"I shot someone man....I ....there was....blood....I ...only did it to protect her...like he told us to." TJ was scared, he had never used his gun before and was starting to hyperventilate.

Taz sat in the car listening to his younger brother give him the details. He knew Truth's being shot would send Trigger on a murder spree.

"Ok calm down lil' bro, I got this. Whateva you do, don't call Trigger. Just you and 'Quena go home and stay there. The police are gonna look for you to ask questions. I'll quiz Iesha on an alibi."

"Man I aint never shot no one. I don't know if that girl lived," TJ said. He was definitely not a killer.

Taz put his car in drive and tried to coach TJ as best as he could. "Look, take the car to my spot and switch cars. Go to Iesha's and chill, I'll deal with this." Taz knew TJ was not cut out for that lifestyle. TJ was more the silent type. He never got into any trouble and had good grades throughout school. He had been with Shaquena since Junior High School.

"You cool bro,' you know I got you," Taz reassured him

"Yea I know," he had his head in his lap thinking about the girl hitting the pavement.

"Do what I said aight? I'll handle Trigger on this,"

"Aight. One,"

"One," Taz said and hung up the phone.

The ride in the ambulance was a blurr. Truth couldn't hear anything. She kept seeing herself as a little girl running around both her mom and dad. She saw her own funeral and burial in her head. The paramedics worked to stop the bleeding. She saw her pregnancy come and go. She tried to look at Taysha who was by her side crying. She suddenly felt warm and everything went black.

Trigger's cell phone rang. "This betta be important, I *am* working," Trigger snarled into his cell phone. He hated to be bothered when he was on the grind, since it threw him off.

"Tavarius, it's me," Zantranelle, his Aunt said.

Trigger stopped and his heart skipped a beat. The last time he heard from his Aunt was when he found out his parents were killed twenty years ago. "Auntie Zant, whats up?"

"Your daughter Truth was shot and the hospital been calling everyone they know. Somehow they got me and I wanted to let you know. Now I may be old but I know you. Don't go seeking revenge and get yourself killed, we done had one too many funerals. Just go be a father to that baby and set her straight." His Aunt was getting concerned about all the rumors she kept hearing surrounding her only sister's son.

He was bothered by her comments but he was truly worried about his daughter.

"Do you know what hospital she is at?" he jumped in his Lexus Coupe and sped off.

"She is at Sinai."

"Ok thanks," he closed his cell phone and sped to the hospital.

Taz was sitting in the waiting room with Aneedra and Taysha who were holding on to each other for comfort. He kept thinking how much he really wanted to get out of Los Angeles and move down south. He saw his father come rushing through the door. He never seen Trigger so worried before and thought he had actually seen tears in his eyes.

"Where she at? What the fuck happened?" he came at Taz with several questions.

The doctor was coming down the hall at the same time Legacy came flying through the door.

"Where is my baby? Oh Lord, where is she?" Legacy ran

over to Trigger.

"Excuse me, are the parents of Truth Morrow here?" the doctor asked

Trigger and Legacy looked at each other and prepared to hear the worst. "We are," they said in unison.

The doctor walked over to them to give them the update on Truth's condition.

"She is in stable condition. The bullet bypassed her heart and punctured her lung. We were able to stop the bleeding. Now it's just a matter of time to see if her body is able to break through from the trauma."

Legacy started crying. She couldn't believe what she was hearing.

Trigger couldn't handle what he had heard and walked out the door.

"What about the baby?" said Tommy who had walked up catching the tail end of the results. Taysha had called him on the phone on the way to the hospital.

Legacy turned to see who had asked the question.

The doctor nodded his head and checked his chart. There was no record of a pregnancy listed. He was concerned at the mention of a possible fetus and wanted to check the status of the baby as soon as possible.

"I'm sorry, no one said anything about her being pregnant. I will have to have the neonatal team come down and check the fetus for any signs of trauma." The doctor walked away.

Legacy stared at the young man in front of her and became upset. She knew there was no way he could be around her daughter's age.

"I am Truth's mother and who would you be?" she asked him

"I'm Tommy, her boyfriend."

He went to take a seat beside Taysha and Aneedra.

Legacy was not willing to settle for just a name, she needed more information.

Walking over to him she sat down next to him.

"Look here, I need to know how old you are and if the baby my daughter is carrying could be yours?"

"I'm 21 and yeah that's my baby she gonna have." He casually grabbed a magazine.

"Did you say 21? Oh my Lord." Legacy was speechless. She was more in fear of what Trigger would do once he found out.

Trigger had come back in the waiting room followed by Taz and caught sight of Legacy sitting next to some young boy wearing a platinum cross around his neck.

"The doctors are checking for signs of the baby now and they will be back with the results. I'm starving, are you hungry?" Legacy was trying her best to keep Trigger from questioning Tommy about anything.

"Naw I aint hungry, who is this?" he pointed at Tommy.

Legacy stepped between Trigger and Tommy and tried to introduce them nonchalantly.

"Trig, this is Truth's friend, Tommy."

"Tommy, this is Truth's father, Trigger,"

Tommy stood up to shake his hand and Trigger's eyes turned stone cold. He knew this had to be the same connect that his guy was trying to set him up with and the same New York cat he had heard about.

Grabbing his hand and holding it with all of his might Trigger said, "Don't think for one minute I wont fucking kill you. I know your type so you betta disappear and soon, before you start something you not capable of finishing." He looked at Tommy with murder in his eyes. Confused, Tommy frowned and removed his hand from Trigger's death grip. He had never met Trigger in his life and didn't know why he was coming at him like he was.

"I'm sorry yo, but I think you got me confused wit' someone else."

"I don't have nothing confused muthafucka, you gon get got if you don't leave this bitch right now." Trigger's voice escalated causing the nurses to turn their head and several other people to stop what they were doing.

Tommy still confused, did not back down.

"Look, I understand it's your baby girl but I been with her for the last month now and that's my child she got in her."

Trigger's anger multiplied after finding out that Tommy was responsible for impregnating his daughter.

"Sorry son, but you wrong there. That's my baby Truth carrying." Dame walked up to them. All three of them turned to face him.

He had received the news that Laquetta tried to kill Truth and he heard about the pregnancy from one of his boys who was fucking Truth's best friend, Taysha.

Taysha and Aneedra looked at each other at the drama before them.

"Who the fuck are you?" Asked Trigger

"Yeah," said Tommy

"I'm Dame. Truth and I were together about two months ago and well, I know for sure that's my child she is carrying."

Tommy was speechless, he didn't know what to say.

Taz was watching the scene unfold and feared the worst when Trigger turned his back. Getting up to walk by, he exited out of the emergency room. He knew if Trigger turned his back it wasn't to calm down.

In one swift turn Trigger had pulled two guns from his waist and pointed them at both Dame and Tommy.

Legacy jumped up and tried to stop him by grabbing his arm. "Trigger don't do this. They just kids. I'm sure we can talk this out."

"Get the fuck off me Cy, you already know the deal." He shot her a look.

Legacy backed up not wanting to interfere but she also didn't want Trigger to make a mistake. She knew he was following the creed; if you pull a gun out you better use it. Several security officers came running down the hallway. Dame tried to move but was struck in the arm by the bullet intended for Tommy. Tommy pulled his gun from his waist and fired back striking Trigger in the abdomen. Doubling over from the pain, Trigger squeezed one more shot from his gun hitting Tommy in the neck. Both Trigger and Tommy dropped to the floor. Legacy was screaming at the sight of all the blood coming from Trigger's side. Nurses and security personnel were everywhere. The police arrived on the scene not knowing who to take into custody due to all the injuries present. Taysha and Aneedra were questioned back and forth as to what had happened but neither one told the real truth on who shot whom. Trigger was treated for his wounds in the Triage while Tommy was rushed into emergency surgery. Dame was released after two hours for his flesh wound. Legacy sat in the room with Trigger just shaking her head.

"You gotta stop this bullshit. You know they gon take you to jail, don't you? You getting too old for this gangsta' shit. You got boys that look up to you and a daughter who needs guidance on what type of man to choose. She keeps choosing these thug ass niggas cause that is what she sees in her daddy. Trig, you 33 years old." She got up and paced the room.

Trigger just lay quietly watching her. He knew Legacy was right, he did need to get out of the game and be a father but the only way out was death. He was not going to go on without a fight. The doctor came into the room with a worried look on his face. He had heard about the incident and thought it was a shame.

"I have information on your daughter's condition." Both Trigger and Legacy turned around to face him.

"She is now awake and trying to breath on her own. Unfortunately we couldn't save the fetus due to all of the blood loss so we had to perform an abortion. If you want you can see her now." He directed his last statement to Legacy. He knew once Trigger's wounds were stable the police would be taking him into custody. After the doctor left the room Legacy turned around and faced Trigger once more.

"This has got to be the end of this bullshit. Or it's your funeral we will be attending. You aint young no more and these niggas are smarter now. Like you told me, you better than this shit, get it together." She turned around and walked out of the room.

Trigger lay in the bed. For the first time since his parents had died he decided to try praying. He knew that if that boy didn't survive it would be an all out war with his boys. This was one he was sure even he wasn't strong enough to handle. He vowed to get out and lay low as soon as he could. The well being of his children was now more important to him than money. If it was the last thing he did he planned on putting it all in the past and starting over.

As Legacy walked down the hall to see her daughter she got a bad feeling in her stomach about the boy that Trigger had shot. From his accent she could tell he was from New York. She had heard plenty about people from New York and knew that even though the east coast/west coast drama had died with Biggie and Tupac, some niggas still carried hatred in their hearts. The way the boy looked and dressed she could tell he had money and that whomever his friends and family were they would be coming back to look for the person who shot him if he didn't survive. Legacy paused for a moment before going in the room where Truth lay. She said a quick prayer and asked God to watch over her daughter in the event something may happen to herself or Trigger. She noticed a young man who looked to be about 19 watching her from the hallway. It was something familiar in his eyes that she seen that she couldn't place. Dismissing it without a second thought she stepped in to Truth's room.

CHAPTER FIVE

SHED SO MANY TEARS

In the intensive care unit Truth stirred underneath all of the tubes that were hooked up to her mouth and nose. She felt like she had been a connect sleep for a long time. She turned her head and noticed her mother standing over her praying and holding her hands. Moving her hand she touched her. Legacy looked at her only child and smiled.

"Hey Truth. How ya feelin'?"

Truth tried to speak but couldn't move her throat. She squeezed her mother's hand and blinked. Aneedra and Taysha walked in the room looking worn out from the long hours they had spent waiting to see her.

"OH, Truth, I'm so glad you are awake!" Taysha said as tears streamed down her face. She was worried Truth wasn't going to make it.

Truth tried to smile but her face was swollen from the bruises she received from the fight with Laquetta. She thought about the baby she was carrying and tried to rub her hand over her belly. She felt like she was empty inside and knew in her heart she must have lost the baby. Looking at her mother's face told her all she needed to know. She wondered why

Tommy hadn't showed up to see about her. After about two hours both Aneedra and Taysha decided to leave and check on her later. Legacy just stood by the bed holding her hand.

"You know I never thought I would be in the hospital seeing you like this. I remember when you were born and I held you. I looked into your eyes and I didn't know what to do with you. I was about the same age as you. Young, and stupid too. Your daddy didn't make matters any betta, cause he was so fine." Legacy laughed as she reminisced.

"When we had you we were babies ourselves and didn't know what the hell to do when you cried. I remember sitting there for an hour straight just staring at you. Your daddy too, I caught him a number of times holding your little hands." Legacy rubbed Truth's hair. Truth lay there wanting so bad to hug her mother. She was hurt by all the pain she had caused her parents. She made a silent vow to try and be better in everything once she was released.

• • •

On the other side of town

Three men sat in a Lincoln Continental smoking weed and drinking.

"Man ya'll hear what happened to T-bone?" One man with dreds said.

"Naw nigga, what happened?" asked the chubby one as he took a pull from a blunt.

"Shit, ma nigga gone, son. That nigga got murked at a fucking hospy by some trick's daddy. The shit was mad ill, yo. Word is that the nigga fell for the okey doke the broad ran on him about carrying his shorty and turned out it wasn't even his, kid, and the bitch was only 17."

"DAMN!!" both guys said together.

They sat in silence for a moment.

"Man, I know Chunky and Bo gon handle dey business on that nigga who killt 'em." The little one said taking a swig from his Hennessy bottle.

The man with dreds shook his head again.

"Naw son, we been hired to do that shit. Chunky said he'll give $100,000 to bring that nigga down. I'm just running it by ya'll niggas 'fore I agree." He looked at his crew for their reaction.

Drunk and high, the crew contemplated for a minute before agreeing to the deed. They were known as the *Silent Head Splitters*, hired by the grimiest niggas to lay bodies down.

"Damn, that's $33,000 a piece. I need me some new kicks too and my bitch finna drop her load in another month. I'm wit' it." Said the chubby one.

"Yeah me too, son. I been eyeing this new bike and mom's finna have that surgery so she can stop having all dem fucking bebe kids. I swear my muver like super fertile, joe." They started laughing. The little one was only 18 years old with ten brothers and sisters underneath him.

They made their plan to take Trigger down in two weeks when everything died down, that way he would least suspect it.

After being released from the hospital Truth had received word about what her father had done. She moved back in with Legacy to give things time until the drama died down. Taysha was right by her side helping her along the way. Trigger had to spend the first few nights after his release in jail until he paid the $10,000 bail money which he had Tasty drop off the next day.

He laid low as much as he could for those seeking revenge on him for killing Tommy. Truth was hurt beyond belief that her boyfriend was dead. She wept for him and her lost baby even though it wasn't Tommy's. Even though she was now eighteen she felt like she had seen so much in her lifetime to write a book. Tommy's funeral was being held in New York since that's where he was from and Truth had to make arrangements to fly out there. She took the money they were saving for the baby totaling about $15,000 from the safe from the apartment they shared and bought plane tickets to New York for herself and Taysha. Boarding the plane Truth turned around and looked at her mother's small petite frame as she stood by.

"Momma, do you wanna go?" she asked.

Legacy was not prepared to leave at all nor did she have anything to hold her back from taking a trip.

"I don't have any clothes Truth, you know that."

"I got you ma, come on, I need you now." She was learning to show her true feelings. She walked back to the ticket counter and bought her mother a ticket. She had planned to scour out New York to see if her mother would fare better there. She was afraid she might have a relapse even though she had been clean from drugs and alcohol for a while.

All three boarded the plane to LaGuardia airport in New York. Once they arrived they were greeted by, Tomisha, one of Tommy's sisters.

"Thanks so much for coming Truth, Tommy would have wanted you to be here." She hugged Truth and gave her a kiss on the cheek.

Truth arrived at Tommy's mother's house and was amazed at how well off his family was. The house was located in SoHo, one of the much nicer neighborhoods of New York City. The foyer was what separated the living room and dining room from each other. In the living room there was a big picture of Tommy sitting by the fireplace. Several of his family members were gathered around the picture talking and mingling. Truth and her mother walked in and the room became quiet. She heard the whispers and all the stares began to burn her skin. She overheard one of the older ladies say, "That's the girl he was with when he was killed. She has the nerve to show up here like her daddy ain't kill him. PUNTA!!!!!" she yelled and was escorted out of the room.

Truth dropped her head and her mother coached her quietly. "Don't be ashamed Truth, you didn't do nothing but love this man and you are here to show your respect. Don't let them take that away because of your father." Truth swallowed down the tears she wanted to let fall and continued walking through the room to get to Tommy's mother. She located the woman she had heard so much about and slowly approached her. His mother was of Haitian and Phillipino descent. She had creamy milk colored skin and long flowing black hair.

"HI! I'm Truth…" Truth stumbled the words out nervously.

"Oh yeah Truth, I heard about you. You the young girl from Cali that had my son smitten for awhile. Well I must say from what I have heard you are quite the brave one to come here and I do respect you for that." She touched Truth's shoulder.

Legacy stood in the background hoping her daughter didn't crumble under all the uppity folks, pressure with their noses high up in the air. Taysha remained in the background taking a seat in the living room. After an awkward moment of silence, the family went back to talking and left Truth and her mother to talk to one another. Legacy decided to approach the question she had been meaning to ask for quite some time.

"So, why did you lie to that boy about ya age and the baby?" She looked into Truth's eyes, seeing herself all over again.

Truth didn't want to answer the question at all. She wasn't sure herself of all the things she had done and why. She knew she was going to try and make some changes in her life starting with her relationship with Trigger.

The next day at the funeral home Truth, Taysha, and Legacy sat in the second row right in view of the casket that contained Tommy's body. Truth couldn't stomach to see him so when it was time for the body viewing she held on to her seat refusing to get up.

"Truth now, come on chile, you gotta put closure to this and seeing the body will help ya." Legacy was pulling Truth out of the chair. She shook her head and held on to her chair causing it to fall creating a loud noise. Everyone was now looking at Truth frowning. Legacy was trying her best to keep her own composure before she said, "If you don't stop acting like a baby I am gonna treat you like one and carry ya ass up there, so get up."

Truth reluctantly rose to her feet and smoothed down the black pants suit she had on. Adjusting her dark, sunglasses, she walked next to her mother as they approached the casket. She looked inside, and Tommy's pale skin was ashen colored and he looked like he was smiling. This was eerie to Truth because she had never seen a dead body after it had been pumped full of embalming fluid. She touched his face and jerked her hand back at the feel of his cold skin. Immediately she felt weak and collapsed at the foot of the casket. Taysha and Legacy helped Truth up and dragged her to the hallway.

"Pull it together chile I know its hard but these folks been staring at you and they expect you to act a certain way. If they don't quit looking at us like that I'm gonna get 'bout it up in here. Uppity ass folks; How the hell you get caught up wit' a rich nigga anyway?" Legacy was smoothing her clothes down.

Truth stood straight up as she watched a young girl that was pregnant stroll to the casket with a child in her arms. The girl was Asian and Black which explained her slanted eyes and long, black hair. The girl studied Tommy's body and bent down to kiss it. Tommy's sister stood up and yelled out,

"What the hell you doing here Tiffany? You know you wrong for showing your evil ass here." The girl burst into tears.

Tommy's family started shaking their heads and whispering. Truth frowned, she wanted to know why they hated this girl so much. Truth left her mother's side and walked over to the girl who was dressed in a black dress covering up her swollen belly. She looked into her eyes and spoke to her.

"How do you know him?" Truth asked

The girl looked at her with tears in her eyes and a smile on her face. "He was my husband. This here is our baby, Kamikaze, and the one I have in my stomach is his also." She turned back and just stood there staring at him.

Truth felt stupid, she never thought about Tommy having a wife nor any kids because he never mentioned them and she never asked. She thought back to the phone call the night of her birthday and realized that it was Tiffany who must have called.

"I knew he was seeing you Truth. Said he was gonna leave me for you." Tiffany shook her head, as the tears fell, she let go of the little boy's hand and turned to Truth.

"You see, I had just found out that I had HIV and I contracted it from him. He doesn't think so and never went to get tested. He left New York to run away from the issue. I knew though that God would bring him back and he did. She pointed to the casket and shook her head. Whispering to the lifeless body she said, "Nothing but death can keep me from it." Spitting on his body she turned and walked away as his family screamed out in disapproval, fighting their way to get to her.

Truth just walked back to her mother. She didn't know what to do or say. She had heard of HIV but never did she think she could be a possible candidate for it. She had only been with two people. She was sick to her stomach and needed to leave. She refused to tell her mother about what the girl told her and remained silent on the ride back to their hotel room. Lying across the bed all she thought about was being tested as soon as she could but she was scared of the results. All she thought of was death. Truth was ready to take her own life right there in the hotel by jumping off the balcony. She stood on the ledge and contemplated jumping for about an hour before Taysha caught her.

"Truth, are you crazy? What the fuck are you thinking?" Taysha had come in looking for Truth only to find her standing on the balcony.

Truth looked at her friend and just started crying. Taysha had seen her go through so much it was unbelievable how strong their bond was. From the murder of a boy, to the clinic finding out she was pregnant; now at the funeral of a boy her dad was responsible for killing.

"I can't live anymore Tay, I may have HIV. That girl at the funeral was Tommy's wife and she said she had it and got it from him. Well he and I didn't use a condom at all. I don't know what to do." She said after she jumped back down to the balcony floor.

Taysha just shook her head at her friend whose troubles were becoming more than enough. "Look, maybe she was lying. Don't believe erything you hear. She was probably hatn' cause you was wit' Tommy." She put her arm around Truth for reassurance.

"Look, we can both get tested together if it will make you feel better when we get back to LA." Taysha looked at her for an answer.

Truth smiled a half smile and nodded her head thankful she

had a friend like Taysha.

•   •   •

Legacy sat in the hotel lounge sipping her Orange Juice wishing she could add a little Vodka to make it more enjoyable. She reflected over the events her daughter was going through and knew that it was only the beginning. She recalled all the things that Trigger had put her through with his women and his gangster ways. She wanted so much better for Truth. Signaling for the bartender Legacy paused before ordering two shots of Vodka. Quickly downing them before Truth came downstairs she felt the warm liquor spreading through her body. She looked around seeing all of the people coming in and out of the hotel with their fancy suits on, all of them looking like they had money.

Feeling sorry for her own lack of wealth she ordered another shot. She noticed a handsome man watching her from the back of the bar. Not wanting to be forward by approaching him and realizing she hadn't made love to a man in over a year, she let the Vodka swallow her shyness. Legacy approached him, gave him her sexy smile and said, "I couldn't help but notice you staring at me. Do you see something you like?"

The man licked his lips and ran his hand over his crotch. He was in town on business and wanted to get him a little something before heading back to his boring wife.

Extending his hand he replied, "Well I definitely do and if you name ya price I can make it worth your while."

He rubbed his chin.

Legacy was overcome by her intoxication and didn't realize he just offered to pay her for a quick nut. She grabbed his hand and rubbed it across her breasts. He smiled and stood up revealing his erection. With not a care in the world she led him to the bathroom located in the back of the bar. Entering the men's restroom she locked the door and propped up her leg. He pulled out his dick and went to insert it before she stopped him. "Hold up partna. You betta strap up, I don't know you like that."

The guy grabbed a condom from his pocket and slipped it on. He tried again and this time she held on as he penetrated her gently at first then increased his motion with force. He picked up Legacy and put her against the door ripping her shirt to expose her breast.

"Yeah you fucking hoe, I am gonna fuck the shit out this pussy here." He drilled her even harder.

Legacy just held on as he had her pinned against the door and rammed into her with such force she thought his dick was going to come through her back. Tears were streaming down her face as she came several times. With each thrust he became more violent biting her nipples and pulling her hair. He put her down and flipped her over as he rammed her from the back. She screamed out more in pain than pleasure.

Knocks could be heard outside the bathroom door as personnel and security were trying to find out what was the commotion going on in the bathroom.

Truth and Taysha had come downstairs with their luggage ready to catch a cab to the airport. She looked around for her mother in the spa and in the gym room with no luck. She asked the front desk receptionist if she had seen her mother and the lady shook her head. A little man about 4 feet tall waddled over to her like a penguin. He looked like a dark version of Webster. He tapped Truth on the thigh.

"Hey there cutie, can you tell ya momma I'm next? She doing the damn thing wit' my boy in the bathroom." He smiled.

Truth kicked him in the stomach and ran over to where a crowd was now gathered outside of a bathroom in the back of the Hotel's bar. Pushing her way through it she knocked on the door. There was no answer so she beat on it.

"Ma are you in there?"

Legacy was laying on the floor with blood pouring from her vagina as the guy stood above her and urinated on her. Pulling two crisp one hundred dollar bills from his wallet he threw them on her and spit.

"Fucking slut, and to think Trigger thought he had a jewel when he was fucking wit' you. That nigga gon learn that he should have never crossed me." He turned her face over as she tried to focus in on him. "Make sure you let him know that we gone get him if we gotta fuck everyone including ya'll fine ass daughter." Dude zipped his pants up and exited out the bathroom window.

Legacy couldn't move. The door was kicked in and security rushed in.

Truth screamed and ran to her mother's side.

"Oh my God, what did you do? Who did it momma? Oh my God, please, get an ambulance. Oh shit ma, what the fuck happened to you." Truth was hysterical. She noticed the money sitting on her mother's thigh and frowned. The scent of sex and urine filled the bathroom. The police had arrived and began their questioning. They made every male that checked in the hotel come down for questioning. Legacy couldn't really give any details for the liquor had clouded out her memory. Truth just stood by and watched as the paramedics examined her mother. She had many questions burning in her head. She moved to the side and let the paramedics do their job. Legacy just sat there unable to look her only daughter in the eye. She knew she had fucked up again and was saddened that she let her lack of sex and her desire for alcohol put her where she was. After being treated for minor abrasions to her vagina she was okay'd to stand up and leave. Truth held out her hand and her mother took it, neither one of them mentioned it to Taysha.

At the hotel next door; a man flipped open his cell phone and made a call to LA.

"Yeah, ma nigga hit that shit bloody. Lay low for a minute out there until they get back and dude get word of this. The lil brat wit' her too. We gon make sure he know who the fuck he done crossed. I'm on the next red eye out there then them bodies' gon drop. Yup, One ma nigga." The man closed his cell phone and jumped in the cab waiting on him outside.

At the airport Truth watched Legacy as she stared into space. Somehow she knew the encounter her mother had was something that had to do with her father. When she got back in town she was determined to find out and get to the bottom of things.

CHAPTER SIX

IF I DIE BEFORE I WAKE!

Back in LA

Trigger was sitting in his beach front house with his girl, Twinkle, and their two pit bulls, Butch and Cassidy. He was reflecting on the events in his life and all the information that had come back to him. He heard about Legacy being raped by a guy that was related in some way to someone he killed. For all the lives that he took the only one that stuck out to him was the very first person he had ever killed when he was just 18 years old. The boy was only 15 years old but he had robbed Trigger of eighteen kilos and he was responsible for coming up with enough money to "re-up" and pay his connect back. He knew the saying that you always remember the first person was true because everyone else became faceless. In his mind he kept killing that same 15 year old boy over and over.

Twinkle rubbed her hand against Trigger's thigh. He turned around to face his woman of the day. Twinkle was 5'8" with dark, ebony skin and a short tapered hair cut. She was a model for Ford Models Inc. Trigger looked into her eyes and shook his head. He had so many women that he didn't pay too much attention to them except the way they sucked his dick or how tight their pussy was. For a split second Trigger thought about settling down with Tasty but he knew the saying was true, you can't turn a hoe into a housewife. Legacy crossed his mind but over the years so much had changed between them that he knew he could never go back down that path either. He lifted Twinkle up and placed her slender legs around his waist. His mind was a million miles away but he tried to focus on the beauty before him. Twinkle felt his cell phone vibrate, reached in Trigger's pocket and pulled it out. She opened it and read the caller ID which said "home". She handed him the phone, quickly got up from his lap and went into the other room.

"Yeah this Trig."

"Daddy? Ummm, this is Truth and I need to talk to you. I know you are probably mad at me but, I, well, I just wanna talk." Truth paused

Trigger was surprised to hear from Truth but was also not ready to show his face so soon around his home until things died down. "Truth, baby girl I am glad you are ok. I'm on business now and well I wont be home for a minute." He walked to the window overlooking the ocean front.

He heard the disappointment in Truth's voice from what she said next.

"Daddy, I know you killed Tommy. I don't understand it but I know it was you. You hurt me and well I just wanted to tell you mommy was raped by some guy in New York. She said he mentioned your name."

The bomb she dropped hurt his heart. He didn't mean for Legacy to get hurt by any means.

"Damn!" he sighed loudly. His anger was rising again but he didn't want Truth to know it.

"Did she get a name or see the face of the person who did it?

"No, but she *is* messed up behind it." Truth waited to hear him say he would take care of it.

"Tell her I'll call her," He didn't say what he really wanted to.

Truth was on the other end crying because she was trying hard to reach out to her father and didn't know how.

"Daddy I gotta go, I'll see ya around"

"Truth wait! Look, you don't understand this life I live and I don't expect ya too. All I can tell ya is to keep ya head up and always trust ya instincts."

"Yea, ok!" She said and hung up the phone.

Trigger was mad at himself for not trying harder to be a father but he really didn't know what to say to her. He paced the floor by the window. Twinkle entered the room and noticed the look on his face.

"What's wrong, you look like you stressing?" she rubbed his head

He just stared at her. She really was beautiful but she deserved so much more of a man than he was.

"Look, I gotta run to make, I'll be back tomorrow." Trigger kissed her cheek and walked past her out the door. Trigger knew Truth. He knew she would be leaving so he headed back to his house to stop her.

Truth was sitting on the floor in her bedroom gathering her clothes to put into a suitcase when she received a call on her cell phone.

"Hello,"

"Is this Truth?"

"Yeah, who is this?"

"Don't worry about all that, just watch your damn back, your father is going to die tonight bitch,"

The caller hung up. Truth just held the phone and frowned. This was the second time she had received a call like that. Looking for her brother, Taz's number, she dialed his cell phone.

"Yo Taz, this Truth,"

Taz was surprised she was calling him. He stopped in the middle of the street on Crenshaw Blvd. "Baby sis, what's good. Man are you cool? You got beef?"

"Naw, but I got a strange call on my cell talking about watch my back and how daddy is going to die tonight."

Taz thought about the same call he had received earlier saying the same thing, only the threat was on his own life. Not wanting his sister to worry he reassured her.

"Don't worry about it, probably some haters. Just keep ya eyes open and remain out of the hood for awhile."

Truth wasn't convinced but she didn't want to press the issue either. "Yeah, ok, well I'll be outta here soon anyway, I'm moving to New York wit' my moms so I can be away from this drama here." She said lying.

"No matter where you go, there is gonna be drama, you just gotta know how to be a soldier and survive the bullshit," Taz knew Truth was naïve to the lifestyle.

"I guess, look, let me get outta here, I have a doctor's appointment,"

"Alright baby sis, stay up and remember what I said," Taz was truly concerned about his sister's safety.

Truth ignored him, she just agreed with him to get off the phone. "Yeah ok, one." She hung up the phone and got up to put her clothes on.

Truth was going to meet Taysha to take the HIV test at the clinic. Hoping for the best, for the first time, she got on her knees and prayed to God asking him to allow the test to be negative and she also promised not to have sex without a condom again. She jumped into her truck and sped off, bypassing the red car that was sitting at the end of the driveway.

Trigger arrived at his house and noticed no that no one was home. His garage was also unlocked. He found this odd because no one knew the code to the garage except him. He pulled his pistol from under his seat and sat it on the passenger seat. He flipped open his built in computer from his dash and pulled up the camera system to the house. Everyone was gone including the lawn maintenance people and the housekeeper. That was highly unusual since he paid them to maintain his house on a daily basis. He wanted to switch cars but felt a strange feeling in the pit of his stomach where he had been shot. Turning his truck around in the circular driveway, he sped off down the street. Glancing back at his computer screen there was a figure that crossed the lawn and went up to the back of the garage slipping inside. Trigger stopped his truck in the middle of the street to watch the person. Whoever it was knew exactly where everything was located including the safe he kept in the lower half of the house. The only people he revealed the location to were his son Taz and Tasty in case she needed money. His anger began to burn as he watched the person break into his safe. Shutting the computer off he made a u-turn in the middle of traffic causing several cars to collide and raced back to his home. By the time he reached his home there were squad cars everywhere, forcing him to park on the opposite side of the street. He watched as the police ran through his home turning everything over until they had nothing. He put his truck in reverse, turned around and drove off. *What the fuck is this?* He thought to himself. He noticed the four car accident that he had caused earlier from when he made the u-turn in the middle of the street. Amongst the pile was

Tasty, whose Black, 2 door, Lexus Coupe was smashed in between another car. Ambulances were everywhere trying to assist those who were hurt. Trigger jumped out of his truck, ran over to Tasty's car and noticed there was blood everywhere. The front end of her car was pushed in and Tasty was trapped between the front seat and the twisted metal. She was conscious but slipping. Trigger tapped on the window.

"Tiosha, please answer me." He called her by her birth name.

Tasty moved her head slightly to the left towards his voice and a single tear ran down her face. She mouthed the words "I love you, take care of my boys," before she closed her eyes.

Trigger beat on the window and ran to the nearest paramedic who could help get Tasty out of the wreckage. By the time they reached her, she was already gone. Trigger fought back his tears. The mother of his boys had died right before his eyes and he felt like death was becoming a regular friend to him. Getting back into his truck he made a phone call to his son. Taz noticed his dad's cell number and was a bit nervous to answer.

"Uh, what up Trigger, what's goin on?"

"Pull over and put your truck in park, son,"

Taz knew immediately something was wrong because Trigger never referred to him as son. Pulling over on the shoulder of the expressway he stopped as he was directed and waited. Trigger took a deep breath as a tear rolled down his cheek. "Your mother is dead. She was killed in a car accident about 20 minutes ago."

Taz dropped his cell phone and hit the steering wheel with his head. He was devastated.

Trigger waited until his son picked the phone back up. Tears were streaming down his face and he could barely speak.

"What.....why.....oh my God, does TJ know?"

Trigger sat in the truck looking over at the ambulances and all of the police cars. He watched them as they used the *Jaws of Life* to release Tasty's body from the wreckage. "No, it just happened, I haven't called him yet."

"Let me tell him, I know where he is. I'd rather tell him in person." He felt his brother would deal with it better if he heard it from him.

Trigger thought about it and decided to let Taz be the one to break the news.

He hung up the phone and sat in his truck with his face in his hands allowing all the pain he felt to come out. He felt like less of a man for crying so he hurried up, dried his face and sped off.

• • •

Taz drove to the house Shaquena lived in. Walking up to the doorway he took a deep breath and rang the doorbell. Opening the door Shaquena stood with a t-shirt and shorts on sporting a pair of black flip flops. Her belly protruded from underneath her shirt. Taz's mouth dropped open at the sight of her stomach.

"What's up Taz, why ya mouth open?"

He pointed at her belly.

"Yeah this our baby, we been keeping it a secret from everyone cause at first we wasn't sure if we was keeping it ,but I'm six months now so it's too late." Shaquena rubbed her belly proudly.

Not wanting to tell her what he really came to say he hesitated for a moment. "Um Quena, you love my brother right?" he asked her.

"What type of question is that? You know this ma nigga fo

sho."

"Would you be there for him even if something bad happened."

She looked at him trying to figure out what he was getting at.

"Did something happen? You seem like something is bothering you."

TJ walked up to the door. "What up Taz what brings you by here?"

"Hey bro, uh… can I talk to you alone for a moment." Taz didn't want to stress Shaquena since she was pregnant.

"Sure, I guess we can go outside. Ay Que, I left you some peach cobbler in the fridge." TJ tried to get her to go inside.

"Whateva, ya'll niggas betta not be talking about no bitch. I may be pregnant but I'll still whoop a bitch ass." Shaquena folded her arms across her chest.

Taz and TJ looked at her. TJ spoke first. "Get your pregnant ass in that kitchen, you be tripping. You carrying my baby and talking crazy." He shut the door behind him.

They both walked to the end of the driveway by where Taz had parked his truck.

"So bro, what's up?"

Taz dropped his head as his heart beat picked up pace. "It's momma," he managed to get out

"What about her? Is she pregnant too?" TJ asked

Taz was trying to find the right words without breaking down but his emotions started getting the best of him. Through tears in his eyes he broke the news. "She's is dead, man. She's…………….gone!"

TJ dropped to his knees and grabbed his stomach as the pain of the news he had received crept up into his chest. He began to gasp for air. Shaquena had been watching from the window and came running out.

"T baby, what's wrong, tell me what's wrong." She was crying as she watched TJ struggle to catch his breath.

"What did you tell him Taz, please, what's going on?" She searched both of their faces for an answer.

Taz just stood there as the tears flowed down his face. He couldn't speak witnessing his little brother's breakdown.

"Oh my God ….my momma……..Lord why ….why her?" TJ was crying out.

Shaquena was holding on to him rocking him as he held on to her for dear life. They both sat in the driveway holding each other and crying. Taz couldn't handle the situation and jumped in his truck to be alone. He wished he had settled down with his lifetime love, Ebony, but because he wanted to please his father and always be like him he lost her when she went off to Ohio State University in Columbus, Ohio. She had even told him she was pregnant but was going to have an abortion when he wouldn't get out of the game. He drove faster and faster until he reached the beach. Getting out he walked along the sand letting all the tears he had for the loss of his mother flow down his face.

Truth sat in the clinic after having her blood drawn to get tested for HIV. She received a pamphlet and a bag of assorted condoms. Taysha received the same thing along with a pregnancy test.

"Girl, if I have HIV I don't know what I'm gonna do. I think I'll kill myself," Truth said to Taysha.

Shaking her head she just put her arm around her friend. "Let's pray you don't have to do no stupid shit like that." Taysha replied

They walked out to Truth's truck and got in. Truth left her

cell phone in her car, she noticed she had several voice messages from her father and her brothers. She frowned because she was afraid to return the calls.

"Something is wrong, TJ called me. He never calls." She looked at Taysha with concern.

"Well call 'em back, heffa, how else you gon find out what's wrong?"

She dialed the number to TJ's cell but the call went unanswered. Truth really didn't like Shaquena so she didn't want to call her either. She was afraid the phone call she had received earlier about her father dying was coming true. Lost in her thoughts she jumped when she felt her cell phone vibrate. It was her mother calling her. Since they had come back from New York, Legacy was keeping her distance away from her daughter due to guilt. Truth on the other hand was trying to reassure her she didn't hold the events against her.

"Hey ma, what's up?"

"Did you hear from Trigger?" Legacy asked.

"No."

"Tasty got killed in a car accident,"

Truth's mouth dropped open as she shook her head. She could only imagine what her brother's were going through which explained all of the calls she had on her phone.

"Oh wow,"

"Yeah, it's sad, but he caused it,"

That caught Truth off guard. "What you mean, he caused it. He who? Dad....I mean Trigger? How?"

"He was in one of his rush modes and made a u-turn that cut some cars off and made them all collide. Tasty was one of the drivers." Legacy didn't too much care for Tasty so her tone was nonchalant and very uncaring. Truth noticed and decided to check her on it.

"Ma, you sound like it's nothing. That's sad my brothers lost their mother. I gotta call them. I'll call you later."

"Yeah well don't get caught up, she aint ya momma. Don't shed tears over a dead hoe."

"That's low. Bye ma." Truth hated Legacy's jealousy when it came to her father and his women. She drove off in her truck to console her brothers and her father.

• • •

A week later at Tasty's funeral there were so many people in the church it was standing room only. Truth learned that Tasty's real name was Tiosha Michaels. In her funeral program it listed that she was a former stripper at the *Candy Shop* down on Layton Ave. After she had given birth to TJ she stopped stripping and started working as a nurse at the hospital where she became loved by everyone. She had saved enough money from working to send both of her sons to college since Trigger paid all the bills. Sitting together TJ and Taz both had on Black Armani suits with dark sunglasses. They sat on the front pew along with Trigger and several other family members. Trigger was dressed in a tailor made Black, Hugo Boss three piece suit. All three men were handsome at their best and very calm. During the reading of the eulogy the pastor mentioned how much Tasty liked to recite the verse *"If I die before I wake I pray the Lord my soul to take,"* whenever she was afraid. Hearing those words had Truth on edge. Her mother refused to come inside to attend the service with her so Truth sat in the back alone. She didn't want to see another dead body close up like she did when Tommy died. After the service was over Truth walked to the front to hug her brothers who were amazingly calm. Trigger was standing next to Tasty's mother holding her up as they were escorted out of the church. She walked to the back away from all of the people lining up to follow the casket being carried out. As she was walking away from the funeral home she was approached by a young guy wearing glasses.

"Smile sweetie, it's not the end of the world." The guy smiled revealing a set of the whitest teeth she had ever seen.

Truth wanted to smile but was only able to frown. Considering the circumstances she was in there was no reason to be happy smile. Truth rolled her eyes, pulled out her car keys and hit the alarm to her truck.

"Oh, so a brotha can't get a smile out of you?" the young man continued. He had been watching Truth ever since she stepped out of the funeral home.

"Look, I'm smiling ok," She flashed a quick fake smile hoping that it would shut the dude up.

Homeboy shook his head and laughed at her.

"You a cocky little something, I can see that now. Well I just wanted to make you smile a little bit. I see you just walked out of that funeral home there and any woman coming out of there needs a little sunshine. So I was hoping I could shine some your way. That's all Ms. Lady." Dude smiled again.

His smile was very contagious and before she knew it, Truth was smiling.

"There you go. See, now was that hard?"

Truth shook her head and smiled again.

"I was wondering if I could have your number and maybe we can do lunch or something?"

"Sure I guess so," She gave him her number and walked away.

Truth started to get in her truck when she saw her father come out the funeral home door in a panic. Trigger was breathing very fast and uncontrollably. Fanning himself he held on to the side of the building for support. Truth was going to jump out and run to his aid when her mother beat her to it. Legacy ran up to him grabbing him right before he collapsed into her arms. Blood began to pour from his backside as he laid gasping for air.

Several people were inside screaming and running around. An unidentified man exited the funeral home through a side door, jumped in a black Expedition truck that was waiting for him and skirted off. Truth couldn't believe it. Her father had been shot while he was at the funeral of his dead lover. TJ and Taz both ran out, guns pointed firing at the fleeing vehicle. People started to exit, running to their cars for safety. Legacy held on to Trigger as he continued to bleed all over the sidewalk.

"Trigger, don't you dare leave me now." She held on with all her strength as the weight of his body pulled her down to her knees.

Truth ran over and fell to her knees right by her father's side.

"Daddy, come on now, stay with us, please, we need you, don't you leave." Truth was crying out to her father as he struggled to hold on.

The conversations around the funeral home were of confusion and fear. Everyone wanted to know why Trigger was shot and who the man was that shot him. Taz and TJ had enough of the drama and vowed to seek revenge on their own terms. Trigger finally stopped gasping for air and his body went stiff. Legacy screamed. Trigger was still breathing but it was as if he fell into a deep sleep. His body was coping with the trauma which slipped him into a coma. The ambulance arrived at the scene ten minutes later and placed him on a stretcher. Legacy climbed in with them. Turning to Truth she looked at her with tears in her eyes. Truth sat staring at her mother for a long while before they closed the ambulance doors. It was then that Truth realized her mother was still very much in love with her father.

"Man, this is some bullshit, on the day of momma's funeral someone comes to gun down my father. This shit stops here, man. I been silent for too long. I sit back and let you do you and watch everything fuck up. NOT NO MORE!!!! I am not going to lose another parent over some bullshit. Them niggas came dirty. Shooting Trigger in the back is like fucking him in the ass man! They took his manhood. That was a pussy ass move they made and I guarantee you someone is going to feel my wrath." TJ was pacing the parking lot as he spoke to Taz.

Shaquena approached him only to be pushed away.

"Fuck off me!"

"Dammit TJ, she didn't do nothing," Taz shook his head. His brother had finally snapped and he knew there would be no stopping him. He was so much like Trigger it that was scary.

"I just came to see if you were riding to the grave site with me or in the limo, that's all," Shaquena rubbed her stomach and frowned.

"Man fuck a grave site, I am tired of crying and saying goodbye. Seeing some dirt thrown on my mom's casket ain't gon do shit for me. She gone. I'm still here, niggas gon know now I'm still here."

"Look man, revenge is sweet but now aint the time. We gotta bury our mother, you know she would never want us caught up in no bullshit about Trigger."

TJ looked at Taz and gave him one of Trigger's *fuck you nigga* looks. Shaquena sensed something different in TJ but she didn't want to anger him anymore than he already was. Taz realized that his little brother was finally coming out of the shell he had been in for so long. He had Trigger's mood swings and attitude down to a science. The killer instinct had even been scratched and now TJ was ready to be down. Taz moved out of the way as he watched TJ look for his 9mm to tuck into his pants. They both had come strapped to the funeral home out of habit. They were used to carrying heat on them since they were 13. Trigger told them to always be prepared for the inevitable. As TJ stomped off to his car Taz looked up in the sky for the first time saying a prayer. He knew with Trigger down and TJ's anger unleashed it was going to be a hell of a year.

CHAPTER SEVEN

AM I MY SISTER'S KEEPER?

"Yo kid, that nigga still breathing, son. We got 'em but we didn't, you smell me? He got two young Joe's too cause they got ta poppn' back, almost made us flip the Yuki tryna dodge bullets." Some New Yorker was talking to his partner while smoking a cigarette. With dreds in his hair he wiped his brow.

"Yo son, A gon fucking flip, kid. We was suppose to have murked that nigga, now he still breathing and them two joe's is gone be on some revenge bullshit."

"Just be cool B. I mean we out on the next flight, we just gon say we did our do and we thought the nigga was dead. Stick to the story. We can't go wrong, son."

"Yo, I 'ont know man. A gon be at that ass once we touch cement. Word life. I'm gone chill soon as we get back."

"It will be cool, don't worry, kid I got A."

"Yeah ok, we'll see."

They both jumped into the taxi that was sitting by the curb and headed for the airport

• • •

Truth was at her mother's house when she received the phone call regarding her test results. The recorded message advised her to come in that day to get her results.

Shaking her head she prayed for the best. It had been two weeks since Trigger was shot and he was still in a coma. Her mother stayed with him day and night. Legacy was more attentive to him than anything else which is why Truth decided to move back home. The apartment she shared with Tommy months ago brought back memories of the baby and the lies she told so she gave it up. She was sitting at the kitchen table, contemplating on whether she should go on her date with the guy she met at Tasty's funeral. His name was Terry but he went by "T-Money". T-Money was six years older than Truth. She knew it was something about him that she should stay away from but she couldn't help being drawn to him. She always attracted older guys and couldn't help her attraction to them. After agreeing to meet him at a nearby McDonald's Truth went upstairs to get dressed. She put on a brown, jean skirt and a cream colored, one shoulder, shirt. She threw on her brown Louis Vuitton sandals and pulled her freshly wrapped hair out of her face with a Louis Vuitton headband. To complete the look she switched her purse to the new book bag style Louis Vuitton backpack she had gotten from her brother, Taz, on her birthday. She checked her reflection in the mirror and looked well over the age of 18. Truth jumped in her truck and headed first to *Planned Parenthood* to get her test results. She walked into the office where a lady pulled her chart and called her to the back. Sitting in the room she thought of all the things she would do if the test, was positive. Truth was nervous and the chill in the room became noticeable. The doctor walked in with Truth's chart in his hand. He looked at Truth and gave her the look of a father concerned about his daughter. Sitting down in the chair he folded his hands together. *I wish he would just hurry the hell up!* she thought. The doctor began to speak.

"Well Ms. Morrow, your results for your HIV test are negative. You are amongst one of the lucky ones. I see you are only 18 years old. I would advise you if you are going to have sex to always use a condom. You have your whole life ahead of you so don't let any one take that away."

He continued to talk to her but Truth tuned it all out. All she knew was that her test results were negative and she did not have HIV. Wanting to get out of his office as quickly as possible she nodded her head to all of the things he was telling her about abstinence and teen pregnancy. The Doctor finally stopped talking and Truth was able to leave. She hurried across the parking lot to her truck so she could meet her date. Pulling into the parking lot she parked and sat waiting on him. After 20 minutes she noticed a white and gold Expedition with 24" rims pull into the lot. Dude's music was so loud he was vibrating the windows of all the cars in the area. His license plate read DROP IT. Easing out of her truck Truth frowned. She had vowed after Tommy died to stay away from men with money but once again she was sucked back in. Smiling, T-money stepped out of his truck and walked up to Truth. He was wearing a white wife beater and some jean shorts, a gold cross hanging from his neck and a big diamond earring in his ear.

"What's good shorty? Why don't you leave ya truck here, jump in mine and we can go get something to eat."

"Ok," Truth locked up her truck hitting the alarm and climbed up into homeboy's Expo.

Inside the interior was tan with leather seats. There were TV's in the head rests and a TV coming out of the CD player.

Dude hit a button on the screen and turned on a movie as he pulled off.

"So tell me Truth, what's your story, I know you got one." He looked at her and smiled again.

Truth had to admit, all the smiling was sucking her in deep. Homey's teeth were so white and well maintained. She felt like she could tell him anything by how comfortable he made her feel. She dropped her story on him from the time she moved out of her mom's house to Trigger getting shot. Dude sat absorbing everything, listening intently. They arrived at a restaurant called *J.T. Bones* which served the best ribs and chicken. It was Truth's favorite restaurant as a child. After talking over a meal, dude kept playfully touching her, slipping every now and then by touching her breasts. Truth didn't notice the first two times but once they were in the parking lot of the restaurant, she caught on.

"Do you think you gon get some cause you fed me? I notice you keep slipping up and touching my breasts." She looked at him.

Dude smiled, grabbed her around the waist and pulled her close to him.

"Look Truth, I like your style, you're simple, not all weaved up like most of these girls out here and you carry yourself with class. You remind me of them girls down in Atlanta who do it all simple. I like you and feel like I have known you forever." He was being sincere with her. Truth grabbed his hand and they started to walk down the beach. They walked hand in hand down the beach, both lost in their thoughts about all kinds of things.

• • •

Trigger stayed in a coma for the next few months with

Legacy at his side day and night. Taz tried to escape his feelings of loss for his mother by trying to turn his own life around. He tried to enroll in a community college just as she would have wanted him to so he could study Journalism and Radio Broadcasting. He gave up after two weeks after he never turned in his homework and began to fail his classes. The money from Tasty's insurance policy allowed him and his brother to be financially set for the rest of their lives along with all of the money she saved for their college funds.

TJ was still on a revenge mission. Living with Shaquena started getting unbearable and he started to follow his fathers' footsteps almost identically. After coming home from a night of drinking and ecstasy pill popping he stumbled in the house. Shaquena was now eight months pregnant and very much fed up with his antics.

"Look TJ, I am sick of your shit. You can't keep coming home like this." She put her hand on her hip and waited for a response.

Reeking of alcohol and smoke, he just waved her off. "Gone wit' that bullshit 'Quena, I'm tired." He pushed by her.

Becoming furious she moved towards him. "You know one of 'dem hoes you fucked called ya celly last night? Uh huh… how you think I know? Because you left the muthafucka here." She threw his cell phone at him hitting him in the head.

Holding his head, TJ picked up the phone from the floor. He knew he left it somewhere but couldn't figure out where.

"Thanks, I was looking for this." He said and started up the stairs headed for their bedroom.

"Gotdammit, T, don't walk away from me when I'm talking to you." Shaquena headed up the stairs behind him.

TJ rolling his eyes, walked into their bedroom and fell across the bed.

His cell phone rang, he was glad it didn't break when it hit the floor. "Yeah this TJ," he answered

"Oh, what up baby. Yeah, I met you last night, you had on that black shirt right?"

"Aw, fo' sho' we'll hook up and I'll give you that,"

Shaquena's mouth was open the entire time as she listened to TJ's end of the conversation. Before he could get another word out, Shaquena hit him upside his head with the lamp sitting on the end table. TJ grabbed his head and noticed blood on his fingers. His mind frame switched and he went into another mode. He jumped up and knocked Shaquena backwards causing her to fall up against the wall. Angered but not one to give up, she bounced back up and punched him in the jaw.

"Fuck Quena, you fucking pregnant, man."

"Fuck you TJ, you fucking hoe ass nigga. I been the bitch here for you when ya damn momma died and ya daddy is damn near on his own death bed." Regretting the words as soon as she said them, Quena stepped back.

TJ swung around fast, pulled his gun on her and placed the barrel up to her temple.

Candace, their next door neighbor, had heard all the commotion and entered their house. She sprinted up the stairs as she heard a gunshot. Shaquena's body dropped to the floor as water spilled from between her legs.

"Oh my God TJ, what did you do?" Candace screamed.

Shaquena grabbed her shoulder and moaned. TJ shot at the wall right past her and the bullet grazed her shoulder.

"My water broke," Shaquena said while trying to sit up.

TJ ran down the stairs to leave.

Despite her injuries and the fact that she was now in active labor, Shaquena got up from the floor holding her stomach and tried to follow TJ. Candace tried to intervene.

"Girl, let that nigga go, he tried to shoot ya ass and you carrying his damn baby."

"I can't, he needs me. He just going through some bullshit right now."

Quena went downstairs after him.

TJ was getting in his truck when he saw Shaquena holding a towel to her shoulder and holding her belly as she walked over to him. The softer side of him gave in because he knew he couldn't leave her in that predicament. He got out, picked her up and put her in the passenger seat of the truck to drive her to the hospital. Candace stood in the door way shaking her head at the both of them.

"Ya'll two should get married cause you are both fucking crazy." She yelled out before she stormed off back to her house.

The ride to the hospital was quiet. Shaquena was breathing through her contractions and TJ was still hung over from the night before.

After several hours of being in labor, Shaquena was ready to deliver. After only four pushes, TJ was able to see his son Tavarius III come into the world. Looking at his son brought a new meaning to TJ's life and he knew he had to do right by him so that he wouldn't grow up to follow his footsteps. He called Truth on her cell phone to relay the good news. She picked up after the fourth ring.

"Damn, hello?"

"Uh baby sis? You busy?"

"TJ? What's up?"

"I just had my son a minute ago. Did I interrupt you?" he could hear fumbling in the background along with heavy breathing.

Truth swatted T-money's hands off of her as she tried to

listen to her brother. They had been sitting in his truck and he had his head between her legs. She was getting ready to have an orgasm when her cell phone vibrated.

"Naw TJ. What's his name?"

"Named him after Trigger"

"You named ya baby Trigger?"

"Naw girl, his name is Tavarius. I think we gon call him Little T for short."

"Oh, ok, well I'll be out there in a minute to see him. Did you tell Taz?"

"No, not yet, he's not answering his cell."

"Well I'll tell him. Have you been to see Trigger yet?" She was curious to know if TJ had stopped by the hospital to check on their father who was still in a coma.

"Truth, you know I aint trying to see him right now. I can't see my man down like that. I'm still gon catch the niggas that did that bogus ass shit. See I don got all worked up. I'm out man." He hung up the phone.

Truth sat in T-money's truck thinking about her brother. T-money was trying to finish what he had started but Truth's attention was now elsewhere. He had pulled out his penis but put it back in his pants and watched Truth from the corner of his eye. She was in another world. She was thinking about her father. She shook her head trying to keep to the task at hand. In her head she kept replaying the conversation she had two weeks prior with Taysha on the phone.

"Girl, they want you to set 'ol boy up." Taysha was relaying the info passed on to her.

"Why, he seem cool and why I gotta do it?" Truth was uneasy about the deal.

"Cause you the one he fucking wit' right now."

Taysha had been informed by her cousin Bunkie that T-money was a big time hustler and had just made a big transaction with a Jamaican named, Aleros. Bunkie being a nickel and dime hustler seen an opportunity to come up and wanted to jump on it.

"I don't know girl, what if something go wrong?" Truth wanted to be sure she was not endangering herself.

"Look, I am going to put Bunkie on the phone and he can tell you the plan." She passed the phone to her cousin who was puffing on a freshly rolled joint.

"Yo, what up baby girl? So you down or what?"

"First off, don't call me baby girl, only my daddy says that and secondly, what do you have in mind? I ain't got time for any bullshit. You feel me?"

"Check it; get that nigga dick wet, right? Then, even if you gotta let him put it in, pussy whip him a little bit and then while he on a sexual high, we gon get him. Just find out where he keeps his safe. I know he got at least a good $32,000."

Truth had thought it over for awhile and thought about the money she could use. Since her dad was still in a coma and her mother was practically living at the hospital, money was tight.

"Ok, how much, and when do we do this?"

"We'll give you 10 grand and as soon as you can, hook up with him." Sitting in T-Money's truck looking at him again, she knew she had to put the plan in to action. She snapped back to reality, climbed on top of him and pulled up her shirt revealing a pink bra. T-money smiled, glad that she was out of her daydream and ready to get down. Kissing his neck and then his earlobes she whispered into his ear.

"We can't do this here, take me back to your place."

Caught up in the moment T-money agreed thinking it would be ok to reveal his home address to her. He felt like he had known Truth for awhile because of how comfortable he could be around her and she never acted like a gold digger. He started up the truck and kept her on his lap as he drove down to a house around the corner from where he had met her at. She kept looking up to make sure Taysha was following without being seen. Arriving at his home Truth turned around to look the house over. She was surprised that it wasn't as big as she expected it to be. She climbed down off of him, pulled her skirt down and adjusted her shirt back into place. The house was a small, one floor, single family home with a porch. T-Money pulled in the driveway and opened the garage door to pull his truck in next to a white Cadillac CTS. Getting out he walked her through the kitchen which she knew was decorated by a woman since there were apple curtains at the windows. He held her hand and guided her to the basement which held a huge king size bed, a 52," Big screen TV, and lots of stereo equipment. One side of the room was decorated with pictures of women sprawled in all different types of positions. Anxious to get her to the bed, T-Money flipped a switch and a red light illuminated the room. Music began to play out sounds of the Isley Brothers *Between the Sheets*. Truth was nervous. She knew she had to keep it together in order to go through with the plan.

She looked at her watch, she had exactly 30 minutes to get her plan poppin and get to the hospital to see her new nephew before visiting hours were over. Taking a deep breath, she walked up the steps to the bed and began to dance seductively removing her clothing one piece at a time. She made sure to hit redial on her cell phone before she put it in her purse so that she could dial Taysha and let her know she was going to do the damn thing. T-money was definitely impressed by Truth and was ready to explore her body when his cell phone rang. Checking the caller ID he noticed it was a text message that read "Trouble in Westside, leave now." Confused, he ignored the message and put it on vibrate as he continued to watch Truth's clothes drop to the floor. She was fully naked across his bed when his phone vibrated again and fell off the nightstand. Grabbing it and looking again at the screen he saw it was his boy "Gipp" calling him. He knew he had to take the call. The only reason Gipp ever called was when a deal went bad or he needed back up.

Sitting on his bed in his boxers he dialed him back. Truth was irritated because time was running out. She tried to stop him by licking his neck and putting her breast on his back. Fanning her off and squeezing one of her breasts, he nudged her to back up. Truth tried to think fast. She had to stall Bunkie and his crew before they came in. While he was on his cell phone she reached in her purse and grabbed her own phone text messaging Taysha the words "He got a phone call, back up for 5 minutes". Receiving the text message just as she was signaling to Bunkie to go ahead Taysha panicked. She didn't know how to stop them after she motioned it was clear for them to enter the house. They were already at the back door when Bunkie received a call on his cell phone. Looking down under his ski mask at his phone vibrating he cursed. He meant to leave it in the car so he ignored Taysha's phone call. He along with two other masked and armed men jimmied the lock to the back door. They were in the kitchen where they could clearly hear T-money's phone conversation.

"Gipp man, I'm busy, what up?"

"Word? Right now?"

"Damn, you always pick the wrong times,"

"Give me like twenty minutes," he looked at Truth who was nervously lying across the bed trying to fake a sexy smile. She heard Bunkie and his crew upstairs when they entered and turned the music up with the remote she found on the bed.

"No, give me like thirty minutes and I'll be through."

"Aight, One"

He placed the phone on silent and turned back around to face Truth. He was ready to feel her body and climbed on top of her. Truth was excited and aroused at the sight of the fine, naked man in front of her. She welcomed him between her legs. She knew even if it was her last time she ever saw him, that she wanted to sample him. Grabbing a condom from the headboard compartment, he ripped it open with his teeth and rolled it on. Truth knew she would be in for a ride by the size of T-Money's swollen manhood. Slowly he penetrated her opening and was able to get in. Bunkie and his crew were checking the one floor house for any signs of his safe. Growing impatient and angry he tried every room including the one that looked like an old lady was a sleep in it. She stirred in her sleep and turned over. One of his boys tried to stand perfectly still but the end of his gun bumped the lamp knocking it to the floor with a crash. Startled, the old woman awoke and screamed at the sight of the two men wearing ski masks standing in her room. While T-money had Truth in a doggy style position, he frowned when he heard his Grandmother scream. Truth's body tensed up and she froze. T-money jumped up naked with the condom still on and grabbed a gun from under the bed. Truth's heart started beating wildly. The old woman was still screaming until Bunkie pulled the trigger and shot her in the arm. By the impact of the bullet, the woman fell out of the bed onto the floor.

"Fuck B, why did you do that? She still alive and that nigga coming up the stairs," Skip said.

"Shit, nigga, she fucking screamed and my finger slipped," Bunkie was nervous. He had never shot anyone up close in his life.

They watched as the blood oozed from her arm. The other man, Terror, entered the room to see what the commotion was.

"What the…" He said as he entered the large bedroom.

T-money was glued to the wall as he scaled the basement wall up the stairs. Truth was stuck. She didn't know whether to get dressed and pretend she didn't know what was going on or just lay there. She grabbed her cell phone and dialed Taysha's phone.

Quietly she tried to whisper when Taysha picked up.

"What the fuck happened? I told you to tell them to pull back, now it's some shit going down upstairs." Truth slipped her shirt on over her head.

"Girl I couldn't stop them, it was too late. Get out of there Truth, my cousin is dangerous when it comes to that shit. I'm sorry I even got you involved in this shit."

"I can't get out, the only exit is upstairs and I am in the basement."

"Fuck." Taysha was scared for her friend's life. She tried to think fast but couldn't come up with anything.

Truth was putting on the rest of her clothes.

T-money heard her whisper when the CD player cut off abruptly.

Truth stopped talking when she realized she could be heard. T-money, naked with a condom hanging on from his now flaccid member, stood with his back on the wall. He shook his head realizing that he had been set up. He crept up the stairs and locked Truth in the basement as he slid in the laundry room adjacent to the kitchen and slipped on a pair of boxers. He could hear Bunkie and his crew trying to figure out what to do. Listening to them argue he could tell this was their first attempted armed robbery. T-money laughed to himself and grabbed his Tech nine located behind the washing machine. Searching for his other cell phone on top of a shelf that he kept in case of emergencies with his grandmother, he dialed his boys Trace and D. Putting the code of 187 in their pagers he alerted them to what was going on. With all three of them in the room with the old lady, Bunkie was arguing about what to do with the other two.

"Damn, fuck this bitch, let's just do her and be out fo' 'ol boy come up these stairs." One of them said.

"We ain't even found the safe. I ain't leaving wit no money, it would be pointless," Bunkie was high and was thinking only about money.

In the midst of their conversation T-money had opened the door for Trace and D who were only around the corner when they received his page. Whispering he said, "These young fucks are so stupid they don't even have a look out, but here they are trying to rob me."

Trace and D shook their heads. They were accustomed to robbing so they knew the rules of the game. Someone was supposed to always watch your back. All three walked to the room located in the front of the house and entered the doorway of the room. Bunkie, Skip and Terror had their backs turned and didn't hear the trio enter the room. They heard guns click behind them and all three turned to find two armed men including T-money standing in the doorway. Shaking his head and heading towards his grand-mother who was lying on the floor, he touched the arm that she was shot in. His anger rose up and he was ready to kill. Turning to face the robbers he said, "I dare one of ya'll muthafuckas to move, and my boys Trace and D will take ya'll out just like that."

Bunkie stared at the two guys he was referring to. They

both had to be about 6'4 and weighed about 400 lbs total. His little 5'9," 150 lb frame would be no match even with his strength training. He tried to think beyond the effects of the weed but just stood still against the wall. He knew one of his guys were supposed to be outside looking out but wasn't sure of his whereabouts. He heard a gunshot and his suspicions were confirmed. He turned to find another one of T-money's boys, Bone, holding his now dead, friends body .

"Look T, this one was trying to escape, guess he won't be going no where now." The guy tossed the body to the ground and Bunkie noticed the guns at his waist side. Fearing for his life he thought about his girl and his mother at home. If he were killed his mother would be devastated. He had lost his older brother to a gang shootout only 2 years before and his mother was still hurt from that. Trying to talk his way out he started speaking.

"Look man…. I'm sorry we tried to rob you….. man we …..was….. see ……we all just wanted some sneakers…man….and well J-Qwon told us you had made this deal and had mad loot…..and ….he gave us….the drop on the spot." Bunkie snitched like a bird. His boys' mouths dropped open at the mention of their long time mentor, J-Qwon who schooled them all in the drug game.

T-money was kneeling over his grandmother checking for a pulse. His anger was boiling over at the mention of J-Qwon's name. They had been enemies for a long time. Since his grand-mother was still alive he dialed 911 on the phone by her bed. After requesting an ambulance he knew he needed to clean house quick. Turning to face Bunkie he walked up to him and snatched the gun he was holding from his hands.

"You a dumb fuck you know that? Ya'll shoulda killed me since you got guns and all. Thought I was gonna be a punk bitch and keep my shit here? DID YOU?" He placed the gun in Bunkie's mouth.

Skip was trying to show that he wasn't a punk. He raised his gun to T-money's temple. At the same time two guns went to his.

"We all might as well die up in this muthafucka cause we aint no fucking punks." Skip said.

T-money looked at Skip and snatched his mask off revealing the face of a young light skinned boy. Skip's eyes never left his.

"You got heart ma nigga, but fuck that. You pulled the gun so you betta shoot it." T-money said to him.

Tears began to roll down Bunkie's eyes as he felt the water run down his leg.

Looking down, T-money started laughing. "Damn, you's a bitch nigga too. Pissin' ya self and shit. Ain't you the leader of this here? Ya'll ain't no damn robbers and you fo damn sho couldn't be fucking with J-Qwon, he'd kill you himself for bitching up." T-money was getting a kick out of torturing them.

In the basement, Truth sat trying to figure out how to escape. After trying the door with no luck, she looked around for windows but they were all block glass. *Fuck, baby girl, think, think!* she thought to herself. Her mind all of a sudden went to the one person she knew she could count on to get her out of this. Her brother, Taz. She called his house and got his voice-mail. She tried his cell phone. Taz was on the phone with Ebony when he noticed Truth's name on the caller id. *This can't be good* he thought. Anytime his baby sister called she was in a fucked up situation.

"Ebony baby, hold on."

"NO Tamaz, tell that bitch to call you back," she was mad about the interruption.

"That bitch, is ma lil' sister."

"Oh,…….. fine. I'll hold"

"Yeah, this Taz."

"Taz," she whispered

"Truth? I can't hear you. Why you whispering?"

"Taz, can you send someone to get me? I fucked up and now some shit is going down that I may not make it out alive from." She made sure to keep her voice down.

Taz had to click over to tell Ebony to hang up.

"Dammit Truth, hold on," he clicked over

"Ebony baby I'm sorry, my sister in trouble, I gotta hit you back," he regretted telling her that.

"Damn, every time one of your siblings call you go running. When are you gonna stop being their keeper? You got a life too you know." She was going to tell him about the son she never aborted.

"What did you say?"

"You heard me. Are you your sister's keeper?"

"Whateva, I'll call you back."

He hung up and pondered what she said before clicking back over.

"Truth, I'm here, where you at?"

"I don't know, all I know is Bunkie is upstairs and I don't know if he is alive. I heard gunshots and I'm locked in the basement."

The mention of Bunkie's name sent a bad chill up his spine. He knew Bunkie and his crew were young thugs who were trying to come up and would put anyone they knew in danger if they could. He had to get more info.

"Truth, how did you get to where you are?"

"I drove wit' T-money," she whispered.

Taz was really angry now. He had warned her about messing

with T-money when he seen her talking to him at his mother's funeral. He cursed his father for being in the hospital. Crossing T-money would make for bad business. Since it was his blood in the middle he had to think quickly. Lose a connect or lose his baby sister and face Trigger once he found out.

"Man, Ok, here is what I need you to do cause T-money is not a fool by far. So if he took you to a house it was probably his Grandmother's house on Layton Ave. If I remember, there is a room in that basement that looks like a closet. Get in it."

Truth did as she was instructed. She found a door that looked like a closet and opened it. Inside were a lot of clothes and shoes of every brand name. She was definitely impressed with dude's style. She shut the door quietly.

"Ok, I'm in here, what now?"

Getting in his truck he found his other cell phone and speed dialed Avery, his close friend and backup henchmen since junior high school who lived in that area.

"Stay put and don't let anyone in. There is a gun in the floor, find it, and take the safety off and hold on."

He put the phone down while he called to give Avery the details on his sister's whereabouts.

Truth was curious to know how Taz knew so much about what was kept in T-money's basement. She found the gun and moved the safety to the off position. She was nervous and shaking. It was the first time she actually held a gun. She knew about the safety and where it was located from Taz.

After securing his boys around the house Taz got back on the phone with Truth.

"Ok, check it baby sis, I need you to come out the closet and shoot the lock off the basement door."

"Taz, hell no, they gone kill me."

He thought about it but dismissed it when Avery confirmed

the location of T-money and Bunkie and his crew.

"They not near you, by the time you shoot the lock, Avery and Danger will be in by then."

Holding two phones to his ear Taz had to listen to Avery giving commands and to the fear in Truth's voice.

Truth was scared and began to cry.

"Truth, stop the water works. You know Trigger wouldn't let you get hurt and since he ain't here I am now. So trust me. I got you."

"I know, I'm just scared is all."

"Yeah, well think of it like this. Once T-money finds out it was you that helped get Bunkie in his house, It's gonna be him or you. Now you decide."

Truth hadn't thought about the notion that T-money would take her life. Wiping away her tears, she stood up and straightened her clothes.

Taz could hear her moving around and knew what he had said would make her straighten up. He listened as he heard her blast the lock off the door.

The noise startled everyone including Truth. T-money had momentarily forgotten he locked Truth in the basement. Squeezing the trigger on his gun, T-Money killed Bunkie instantly splattering his brains against the wall and ducked as Skip pulled his trigger striking Trace in the neck. Terror fired his gun missing his initial target and was shot in the head by D. Skip tried to dodge the bullets D was shooting by rolling around and crashing through the bedroom window. He caught a bullet in the arm and fell out in the grass and started running as fast as he could.

T-money ran towards the door where he saw Truth following Avery. He tried to stop Truth from leaving by shooting at her but he missed. Truth was terrified and squeezed the trigger on the gun she was holding hitting T-Money in the abdomen. Doubling over, he dropped to his knees. Truth was stunned she had actually shot someone. She wanted to go back in to help but was yanked out the door by Avery and some other guy who walked backwards holding a sawed off shotgun to watch their back as they ran to the truck waiting outside. Once inside they floored the gas and drove away. Taz was still on the line with Avery directing him to his whereabouts to bring Truth. She was in shock from watching T-money drop to the ground. She didn't know if she had killed him but she knew after shooting him she would never be the same. They drove her to her brother's truck and she jumped in. Taz shook his head and hugged his sister hard. He couldn't believe how caught up she was getting in the streets. He blamed Trigger for not being there for her. Thinking back on the words he heard Ebony say, he realized they was true. He was definitely his sister's keeper.

CHAPTER EIGHT

DADDY'S HOME!!!!!

Sitting in his truck in Palisade Valley, Taz watched Truth as she just sat staring out the window. He knew if she was true to her bloodline she would never be the same after shooting her first victim and this bothered him.

"What are we gonna do if they retaliate?" She asked

"Fight back, what else?"

"Man, Taz, I fucking shot him in his stomach. I really gotta move now. There is no way he's not going to send his men or a group of bitches after me."

"Truth stop bugging, knowing T-money, he'll want to do it himself."

Truth looked at her brother. "Thanks, you are such a fucking help." She folded her arms across her chest and switched subjects. The time was now 9 pm, she was sure visiting hours at the hospital were over. "Oh …TJ called earlier and said Shaquena had her baby. They named him after Trigger."

"Damn, he named the baby Trigger?"

Laughing because she had said the same thing she said, "No fool, his real name is Tavarius, he's number 3. We should go see them, that might take my mind off this shit."

"Deal, what hospital?"

They drove to the hospital to see their new nephew.

Meanwhile a conspiracy was underway. T-money was in the hospital emergency room recovering from his gunshot wound to the stomach. The fact that Truth had nerve enough to shoot him even after she had him set up turned him on in an odd way. He wanted a ride or die chick like her in his life. He wasn't through with her and would seek revenge on his own time. His partners wanted to take her out but he knew her two brothers and Truth's father would cause a war in LA if they found out. So he told them to chill and he would handle it. He thought about her brother, Taz, whom he had made a lot of transactions with. If he knew the Morrow's he knew they rode down on anyone who crossed them. He laid back in the hospital bed thinking of a plan as the nurse walked in to check on him.

• • •

At the hospital in ICU Trigger stirred in his sleep. He had been in a coma for over three months and had missed the birth of his grandson. Legacy was right by his side reading a book by Antoine "Inch" Thomas called *Flower's Bed*. She was engrossed in her reading and didn't notice Triggers eyes open and looking up at her.

"Le....Leg...a...cyyyy," he spoke her name weakly.

Looking up she screamed. "Trigger, Oh my God ...Oh my God.....I'm here baby." Tears streamed down her face as she hugged his head.

He frowned at her. He thought he had only fallen asleep and felt it was strange she was elated to see him awake. The nurses came running in after hearing her scream. They checked his vitals and called for the Doctor to come in the room to examine him. Legacy was overjoyed. She had put on weight, gaining almost 30 pounds in three months from eating and sitting at the hospital. Her hair had grown out and she was plump. Looking at her, Trigger thought she was pregnant from all the weight she gained. He tried to speak again.

"Leggg.. a.. cyyy? Baaaby?"

Confused at what he was trying to tell her Legacy put her finger up to his mouth to hush him. She wanted to call Truth to let her know he was awake. She decided to wait when the doctors came in the room adjusting all the machines and talking hospital language to her.

• • •

Truth was sitting in her truck with Taysha smoking and drinking. After shooting T-money she was lured into another lifestyle of selling drugs. She didn't finish high school and hadn't been to class at all for her senior year. Her life took a downward spiral. Her brothers were caught up in their own drama leaving her to fend for herself. She had hooked up with one of LA's major drug kings, a dude named "Assault". He met her at Club Connections where she was able to get in with fake ID that said she was 21 years old. It was the only club where all of the ballers hung out. When he first spotted Truth, Assault knew right away that she was Trigger's daughter. She had the same complexion and eyes that all of his children inherited from him. He had to have her on his team. Knowing she was naïve to the game, he planned on using Truth to get to her father and destroy him. Truth was dressed in a red halter dress that accentuated her young body and he had been watching her dance all night from where he sat in VIP.

"That little one right there, go get her." He signaled to one of the bouncers to bring Truth up to him.

Assault was a good looking man. With a caramel complexion and standing at 6'2 and 190 lbs of all muscle, he was a force to be reckoned with. He kept his hair low cut with waves. The dimples in his cheeks and his hazel brown eyes kept the ladies falling at his feet. Not to mention he had more money than anyone his age. At 31 years old he was a millionaire with clout around town. In the streets he was untouchable just like Truth's father Trigger. Walking up, Truth carried herself like she was 21 so as not to tip anyone off to her real age. Her friend, Aneedra followed her and thought it was a bad idea to meet a stranger in VIP.

"Let's not go Truth. I don't know about this one." Aneedra said nervously.

Truth looked at Aneedra and rolled her eyes. "Next time don't come wit' me. You gotta be able to roll wit' the big dogs baby or you'll get shitted on. This here is my chance to shine." Truth was looking to come up. With Trigger being in the hospital and no income coming her way she wanted to regain the lifestyle she had grown accustomed to. Used to being spoiled and getting her way she struggled to maintain her expensive tastes alone. She failed to keep a legitimate job so she sought out money in the streets. Assault watched as she sat down and the look in her eyes revealed her innocence. He knew Truth was no more than 18 years old and smiled at the fact that she had game enough to convince people otherwise. Even though she was a sexually appealing girl he didn't want the thought of sex to distract him from his plan. He had big plans for Truth.

"So what up lil' ma, what's good wit' you?" Assault eyed her while he sipped his Hennessy. He ushered the bartender over to the table. "Ay, get me a glass of Cristal for this pretty lil' thing here," he smiled at her revealing the diamond he had in his front tooth. Truth was immediately caught up. One of Assault's lady friend's named, Mia, grew jealous at the attention he was now giving Truth. She put her hands on her hips and stood up. "I'm ready to go home." She pouted her red lips.

Assault turned and glanced at Mia. She was a beautiful girl he had been messing with for over a month. Mixed with Puerto Rican and Black she could have had any man she wanted but she settled for a drug dealer like Assault who mistreated her whenever he felt like it.

"Look, go downstairs and get you another drink. Don't sweat me." He waved her off and turned his attention back to Truth who was now sipping the drink that was ordered for her.

Mia grew angry by and knocked the glass out of Truth's hand, spilling the expensive champagne on her dress and Assault's shirt.

"I'm not no fucking hoe, you can't tell me to go get a drink and dismiss me like that you asshole."

Without a second thought Assault jumped up, grabbed Mia by her hair and pushed her face down on the table. "Look bitch, I told you don't sweat me, now unless you want to die I suggest you follow my man here and let him take you home." He pushed Mia towards Calvin, one of his sidekicks. Calvin just shook his head at the girl and took her by the arm. He was used to being the one to escort the ladies home, sometimes scoring by acting like he really cared about how Assault treated them. Turning back to Truth he noticed she never flinched or showed a sign of fear. Truth just sat there watching. She had seen people murdered in cold blood so this was nothing to her.

"Do you do all your women like that?" she asked him and wiped off her dress.

Assault smiled. He had underestimated her. "What's ya

name sweet heart?"

"It's Truth and yours?"

"Assault," he said while straightening his shirt.

"Assault? I know damn well ya momma didn't name you that. What is ya government name?"

"If I tell you, I'll have to kill you." He smiled again revealing his dimples.

"Well kill me now cause I am not about to accept that for an answer." Truth crossed her legs.

Looking at her legs and loving her attitude Assault was definitely impressed.

He sat down and moved close to her. Whispering in her ear he said, "My name is really Aquarius Garvey but just call me Assault."

His mint smelling breath was intoxicating. Truth kept her cool so as not to reveal any weakness. She had to get close in order for him to trust her. Taking her hand he kissed it and looked into her eyes. He wanted to be sure not to get caught up so he stared at her. Truth stared back as if she was talking with her eyes. The stare down was broken when Jason, the club bouncer, came to get Assault.

"Yo A, that little number you put out is showing out in the front of the club, take care of it before she go to jail."

Assault narrowed his eyes and got up from the table. He was tired of Mia's outbursts when she couldn't get her way. This was the third time he had to take care of her. He pulled out a card from his pocket and handed it to Truth.

"Here is my cell number, call me, this ain't over at all."

Truth took the card and put it in her purse. Aneedra walked up in time to bump right into Assault as he was coming down the stairs. He grabbed her to keep her from falling.

"Damn baby, I know women always falling in my arms but

you trying too hard."

He made sure she was cool and darted down the stairs.

Aneedra frowned up at his comment and found Truth standing up. "Girl, you hear that cocky nigga? Talking about I'm trying too hard. I didn't do that shit on purpose."

Truth just smiled at Aneedra and walked towards the stairs.

"Bitch you got his number didn't you? Truth! Answer me. He's your type too. You like them cocky niggas wit' money. You a hoe Truth you know that?"

Truth stopped and turned around on the steps, "You hanging wit' me so what does that say about you?"

Aneedra couldn't answer so they both just walked down the stairs. Outside she watched Assault get into his black, Mercedes with Mia who was strangely calm. Mia noticed Truth watching her so she stuck her middle finger up and licked it. Truth shook her head and walked to her truck. She had plans to stay out of Mia's way but she was definitely going to get to as close as she could to Assault.

● ● ●

At the hospital Legacy held on to Trigger's hand. He was wide awake and had many questions burning in his head. He had to go through several therapy sessions to regain his ability to walk. The bullet had graced his spinal cord severing a nerve that caused temporary paralysis. Pushing the button on the bed to allow him to sit upright he looked at Legacy again. He realized she was there every day he woke up and when he fell asleep. He missed his children terribly and not being able to speak to them for three months, he knew there had to be a lot that he had missed. Turning to look at Legacy he decided to ask her the questions he had.

"Have you been able to reach my baby girl or the boys?"

Sitting on the end of his bed Legacy looked down at her shoes. She had received a call from her cousin Boom about three weeks prior. He had mentioned seeing Truth at several clubs with Assault. Legacy didn't know what to do and with Trigger being in a coma for the last three months she didn't know who to turn to. She was sure Truth was in over her head again and didn't want to upset Trigger with any news so she lied.

"I keep getting their voicemails." She felt bad for not even trying to call his children. She didn't even tell Truth he had come out of his coma. Trigger felt bad that not even his sons had come to visit him since he had come out of his coma. He wondered what the word was on the street and knew there was one person he could truly count on to tell him. He asked Legacy to grab him some food from the cafeteria so that he could be alone. Once she left the room he picked up the hospital phone and dialed his main man Burna.

"Yo this B, who dis?"

"Man what's good?"

The sound of Trigger's voice made Burna almost crash his truck. He hadn't heard from Trigg in three months and had assumed the worse when Legacy didn't have any information on him. Taking over, Burna assumed the position Trigger once had making himself the *Go To* man for all of his connects. He had become rich in only two months and the status and the money had gone to his head.

"Yo Trig ma nigga, what up? You aight?" Burna pulled over so he could talk to him.

"Man I can't call it. Just laid up in this muthafucka half way paralyzed and shit but on the real what's good?" Trigger didn't want to talk about his injuries, he wanted to get straight down to business and needed answers right away.

Burna ran down unnecessary information on who shot whom and who got locked up, things he knew Trigger would care less about. Sensing his hesitation Trigger knew something was up so he decided to ask about "Operation T". Burna's answer to that question would let him know all he needed to know. "OperationT" was a plan they had put together to take down the North side's drug connect named "Telly", a Jamaican who was providing Kilo's at half the price the Latinos charged and was lacing it with Baking powder. This was so he got more money for less work. Once Trigger found out how Telly was getting by, he wanted to take Telly out and take over the entire North side.

"So what about Operation T, did that shit go down or are ya'll side stepping getting rich off the boss' hog?"

Burna cleared his throat, he never appeared nervous for anyone else except the man he feared the most. "Well you know business been slow since you been down, them young niggas taking over every corna and block out here. The game is getting crazy but we still on top trying to make it work out." Burna bit his bottom lip waiting on Trigger's response.

Trigger swung his legs to the side of the bed. The feeling was coming back every day the more and more he went to therapy. He pondered for a quick second what Burna had said about business being slow. He knew it was a lie when he seen on the news one of his men "LJ" had got popped outside of a bar while almost being carjacked. The car they were referring to was a brand new Lexus with 20" rims. LJ was a "bottom feeder," hustling for others and only making a third from the profits. Trigger knew there was no way he had enough to buy a brand new Lexus. He knew right away Burna was lying. Deciding he would handle the situation in person he flipped subjects.

"Do me a favor, have Deena call me."

Deena was one of the many women that Trigger kept in contact with on financial matters. She was a bank manager and was very good at keeping all of his money stationery while he was in the hospital. Burna had been trying to get to Deena with no luck. Even though she was married she was faithful to Trigger whenever he needed anything from her.

"Sure thing Trig, say, you keep ya head up. When ya coming out that prison?"

"I'm not sure but you'll be the first to know when I do get out."

"Aight cool, call me, I'll have a car outside waiting for you."

"Aight well I'm medicated so let me get off this horn."

"Aight One."

Trigger hung up the phone and thought about his plans once he was released. His phone rang and it was Deena on the line.

"Hey Tavarius what's going down?"

The sound of his name on her tongue and the sweetness of her voice made Trigger's dick hard. He didn't think he had any feeling in it anymore but was happy to see the bulge in his pants. Smiling he answered her.

"Well Ms. Deena, when I get out of here a lot could be going down."

She giggled. She loved the sex she had with Trigger whenever it happened. Though she was happily married, her husband did not satisfy her like Trigger did.

As he was talking, Legacy walked back in the room with a tray of food and a bottle of juice. Setting the items down she tried to eavesdrop on his conversation. Not wanting her to see his erection he pulled the sheet over his lap. Legacy could hear a woman's voice on the other end of the phone. She grew jealous and tried to interrupt him and make her presence known.

"Hey Bey I brought your food up"

Trigger smiled knowing what Legacy was up to and ignored her.

Growing frustrated Legacy pushed the nurses button by the wall and sat down.

The nurse walked in and looked at Legacy who pointed to Trigger and whispered, "He says he wants a bath or something and he is too big for me to do it myself."

Trigger had his back turned and was unaware of the two big men coming through the door to assist him in the wheelchair. Turning around he frowned at the sight of the men in white trying to lift him.

"Umm Deena, just do what I asked you to do and I'll call you later, something is going on here in the room." He hung up and looked at Legacy who had her face buried in a magazine as if she didn't notice the men come in the room. Trigger declined the bath but the nurse had ordered it already and they had to follow orders. He put his middle finger up as he passed by Legacy's chair and she just giggled.

• • •

Truth was sitting in the living room of Assault's condo on the Upper East Side. Over the past few weeks she had become attached to him learning everything she could about him. He taught her how to bag up the "raw" and would send her in the hood to maintain watch on the others he had working for him. She found out where he stashed most of his money and had even peeped out his gun collection. Assault reminded her of her father in his business dealings. He never took no for an answer and his word was bond. Truth realized people feared Assault the same way they feared her father. The comparison of the two was strange to her and she knew she had to find out the deal behind it. While she was watching BET her cell phone vibrated off the table. She bent down to pick it up when she heard that familiar voice again. Mia had walked in the door. *How the hell she get in here?* Truth thought. She listened to her footsteps as she walked around the condo searching. Truth knew she must have been looking for her so she crawled to the side of the couch.

"I know you are here you young bitch so just come out and talk like a woman." Mia was walking through the condo looking for Truth. She wanted to face her woman to woman and give her a piece of her mind. Truth decided to see what she was on and stood up. Mia's back was turned to her and she could tell something was wrong.

"I'm here, what's up?" Truth asked

Mia turned around and Truth's mouth dropped open. The once beautiful girl she had seen in the club two months ago looked like a crack addict. Her skin was blotchy and she had several bruises on her cheek. Her hair which was once long and flowing was now tangled and matted against her head. She was frail and very thin. "Close ya mouth girl, where my man at and why the fuck you think you about to take him from me?"

"I ...don't know what you are talking about." Truth was still in shock at Mia's appearance.

"Yes you do. You one of them spoiled ass bitches who think they can just find a hustler and life will be all good. I worked hard for Assault. I cleaned tables when he didn't have anything. I put him on with my checks I used to get from stripping."

"Yeah and she sucked dick when she could just so she could get close to me." Assault added. He had walked in while Mia was talking. Both of them turned around to face him. Assault was wearing khaki slacks and a white dress shirt. His diamond earrings sparkled from his ears and his hair was freshly cut. Truth was salivating over him and wanted to sleep with him. He kept turning her down saying it was business before pleasure. Mia turned her nose up and crossed her arms over her chest.

"Oh and lookie here, we have the nigga of the hour in all his muthafuckn glory. I want my money Assault or I'll tell ya little tramp everything I know about ya trifling ass."

Assault walked over to Mia and stood in front of her. His body frame was much larger than hers. He looked down at her causing her to take a step back. Truth watched the interaction between the two as they stared each other down. She didn't understand it but she was going to stay until she found out.

"I advise you to get out of my house now and leave my damn key. I don't owe you a penny, remember, we discussed this a long time ago." He frowned up at Mia.

"Nigga, I am not just some hoe and you keep treating me like one. You cut your own damn son off when you stopped the checks coming to my house." Mia started crying.

Assault just stared at her.

Truth frowned at the mention of a son. He didn't tell her he had any children.

"Mia check this out, I told you if I caught you basing up again I was going to cut you the fuck off. I seen you go into the Enterprise just the other day." He shuffled through the mail on his kitchen table.

Mia was determined not to give up, "Well if you don't start taking care of us again I'm going straight to the feds about your plan to take down…." Mia's last words never came out. Assault pulled a .45 from his waist and shot her in the head. Her body dropped to the ground instantly, blood spilling out everywhere. Truth was too scared to scream and froze in place as she watched Mia's body twitch and move. Hearing gunshots, Calvin came running in the door and stopped at Mia's body.

"Damn…what the fuck happened here?"

"She threatened me. No one threatens me." He turned to Truth. Walking over to her he calmly grabbed her hands and kissed her cheek. Truth's eyes were big, she didn't understand how someone could kill someone else and not feel anything.

"You hungry? I'm starving, why don't we go to Prime Quarter Steakhouse and then catch a movie?" He was looking at Truth while caressing her face. She agreed, afraid to tell him no. He headed out the door to his car. Calvin picked up a plastic bag and put on gloves as he tried to pick up Mia's body. Grabbing her purse as she headed out the door Truth saw something that turned her stomach. As he was placing Mia's body in a bag her small belly was protruding out. Truth could tell she had to be a few months pregnant and when her arm moved she dropped a piece of paper from her shirt. Truth quickly picked it up and stuffed it in her purse while Calvin's back was turned. She planned on reading it as soon as she could to find out what Mia was trying to say. While sitting in the car her cell phone rang again and it was an unknown number. Not one to answer unknown or blocked calls she picked up and answered anyway.

"Hello"

"Hey baby girl,"

"Daddy?"

Assault turned his attention to her as her face lit up. Truth was overjoyed to hear her father's voice.

"OH my goodness how …..what…..it's good to hear from you!!!! I'm coming right now to see you." She missed her father and wanted to see him. Assault tuned in to be sure he caught all details.

"Truth, I need to know who you are with right now?"

Trigger had caught word that she was kicking it with some guy around the way who was involved in one of the biggest crime sprees in the LA area. He was truly concerned about her well being and faulted himself for not being there to protect her from certain men. Sensing his fatherly protection once again Truth did not want to tell him about Assault.

"I'm with a friend daddy but he is about to drop me off to my car and then I'll come out to the hospital to see ya, ok?"

"I'm about to leave so I'll call you when I get to where I am going .Baby girl you be safe. Life is short and you have your whole life ahead of you. Don't throw that away." Trigger's brush with death made him realize he had to do all he could to save his only girl from the street life.

"Uh dad, please spare me the save the children speech. Call me later." She hung up the phone and choked back the tears that were forming in her eyes. Truth was getting emotional and didn't want to appear weak in front of Assault. He was looking over at her. He had schemed up a plan that would put him ahead of the game. She was going to be his number one player, only she had no idea about it.

At the hospital Trigger had regained full use of his legs and was able to move about without assistance. The doctors' okay'd his discharge request and allowed him to leave as long as he kept up his therapy sessions with the physical therapist. He knew going home would be a challenge. He hadn't been to his house since Tasty's death and didn't want to return to the memories at all. He retrieved Taz's new cell phone number from his pocket and called him.

"Speak it," Taz answered

"Tamaz?"

"Dad? What's up?", Taz was surprised to hear Trigger's

voice. He had been so busy in his own life he never took the time out to visit him at the hospital. He wondered how he had gotten his number but he was glad to hear from him.

"Come get me son, I'm leaving this hell hole."

"Sure thing I'm on my way."

Trigger hung up and sat back on the bed. Legacy walked in and sat down on the bed beside him. She rubbed his head. He looked up at her and saw the girl he fell in love with over 18 years ago. Legacy was always there through everything he went through. They locked eyes and stared at each other for a long time. The nurse came in the room witnessing the interaction and smiled.

"Looks like you two have a lot of catching up to do when you get home."

They turned away and just shook their heads. Taz walked into the room. Legacy realized how much he looked like Trigger and wished she had kept the baby boy she carried years ago before she aborted it.

"Hey Legacy, what up?"

"Hey Taz, how are you?"

"Aw, you know me, I'm straight. What up Trig? Ya look good as new."

Trigger was wearing a blue jogging suit. His hair had grown out and he was sporting a fro. His facial hair had even grown in.

"Our first stop gonna be the barbershop so you can get all trimmed up cause right now you look like my grandfather." Taz playfully punched him in the arm.

Trigger gathered his stuff and realized Legacy was waiting for him to say something. He wanted to take her to his home and lay her down but he wasn't ready to go there with her.

Rubbing her face he looked into her eyes. "Legacy, thanks

for everything." He kissed her forehead.

Taz stood by and actually felt sorry for Legacy. He knew his dad's ways with women. He would pull them close only to push them away.

"Trigger, I just want you to know that I ...." She stopped, pausing to look at Taz who was standing in the doorway. Taz caught the hint and walked down the hallway.

"I love you and I am here for you whenever you need me."

"Thanks, I appreciate that and I love you too Legacy." He gathered the rest of his things and headed down the hall. He turned to look back at her and saw the tears falling from her face. His heart felt saddened at her pain but he had things he had to handle. Going back home was going to be a challenge and Truth was his first priority. He was going to try and change his ways so that he could be a good father to her. On the way to his apartment Trigger looked up at the sky. The weather was warm and the breeze was still. His mother had always told him when he was little, anytime the breeze blows by your cheek, a change is gonna come. He felt the breeze on his face and knew something somewhere was going to happen. He just hoped it was for the better and not the worse.

CHAPTER NINE

THE SET-UP!!!!!

After being at home for over four months with his new son, TJ was ready to move around. He had grown tired of being around Shaquena's nagging and bossiness. Since she had regained her shape back, she was always leaving him with the baby so she could go out with her girls. Tonight would be the exception. TJ hired a babysitter, his aunt Kasey, to watch the baby so he could get away. During the time he was in the house he put together a plan to get revenge on the people who shot his father. He had his boys Dank and Tip get as much information as they could. They located one of the men who had flown back from New York in a club one night while he was drunk. Walking over to him they pumped four shots in his chest and ran for the door making it out just in time before security realized what had happened. TJ knew there was still one involved and he wanted to get him on his own. Lost in thought he didn't hear the doorbell ring. Finally the persistent ringing brought him out of it and he ran to the door before "Lil T" woke up from his nap. Standing there in a white t-shirt and blue jeans was his father with a fresh hair cut. He looked younger than his 33 years and had shaved his facial hair only sporting a goatee. TJ's eyes lit up. He was happy to see his father was out of the hospital and walking.

"What's good son? Where is my grandson at? Damn ,that sounds weird to say that. You sure making a nigga feel old."

TJ smiled and pointed to the bassinet sitting in the living room.

Trigger noticed TJ was staring at him and was unusually quiet. "You ok son? You look like you seen a ghost?"

"Yeah I'm good. You look good dad.. uhh…. Trigger I mean. Glad to see you is all."

"Don't get soft on me nigga. I don't do the mushy shit you know that. But you can give me a hug."

The two of them embraced. Trigger stood over the baby and looked at him the same way he looked at Truth when she was born. He couldn't believe how much the baby looked like his son. As if the baby sensed his presence his eyes opened and he looked at him. Trigger smiled at him and picked him up. In his eyes he saw Tasty. The same color eyes she had were staring back at him.

"He's got ya momma's eyes."

"Damn, no one noticed that but me!" TJ said. Trigger held the baby close to him picturing the day he held on to both TJ and Taz as babies and now they were grown men with their own issues. He wished he had been more of a father to both of them, rearing them to go to college and make something of themselves.

Setting the baby back down he wanted to get down to business with TJ and find out what had been going on since he had been in the hospital. As he was talking, TJ's doorbell rang. Truth was standing outside anxious to see her father. Trigger opened the door and she jumped into his arms.

"Daddy!!!!!!"

He stepped back and took a long look at his only girl. Truth had put on weight and filled out in the areas that pulled most men to her.

"How is my baby girl?" He said hugging her again.

"I'm better now that you're home."

They talked for awhile longer. Truth was relieved her father was not as bad as she had heard he was a few months before. All three sat reminiscing and enjoying each other's company.

● ● ●

On the South Side

Sitting in his truck T-money contemplated on going through with his plan. He wanted to get revenge on Truth in a way that she would least suspect. He had heard on the streets her father was out of the hospital and with him being back on the scene she would be hard to touch. He had to think of a plan to get her alone with no suspicion. Picking up his phone he dialed the one person he knew could get to her with no suspicion.

"Hello?" the soft voice answered

"Hey girl, what up?"

"Umm not much, who is this?"

"This is T."

"Oh...."

"Yea I got something I need you to help me with."

Sighing, the girl on the other end knew she was risking everything by talking to him on the phone.

"What you need T?"

"Your help. I'll give you part of the profit after the plan goes through."

"How much?"

"$50,000 is what I am trying to cop from it. You down or

what?"

"If I got an idea of what you talking about you know that shit is ill."

"That shit was ill that you did for your cuz but I didn't see you shed a tear over that."

Pausing for a moment she reflected over her dead cousin and shook her head.

"What's the plan?"

"Kidnapping? All you gotta do is be there."

"I don't know."

"Come on now what is there not to know, you gon get $25,000 guaranteed." He was trying to coax her into it.

"Well can you meet me and we talk in person? I don't want to do this over the phone."

"Fo sho', meet me at Checkers parking lot in 20 minutes," hanging up T-money sat back and smiled. He knew there was no turning back now.

• • •

Taz was smoking on a blunt sitting in his truck waiting on his friend, Dub C to come out of his house when he saw Taysha pull into Checkers parking lot across the street. He thought it strange as he watched her looking around as if she was waiting for someone. He figured it must be his sister she was waiting on until he seen T-money's black Cadillac pull next to her. Sitting up he paid close attention to their interaction. Just a month ago Taysha had T-money set up to be robbed by her cousin who was killed during the attempt. Truth had been the bait for the robbery and shot T-money as she was leaving. Taz knew something was up by the way Taysha jumped out of her car and looked around. Hoping she would miss his truck parked across the street he ducked down in his seat so that he could not be seen. He watched as T-money exited his vehicle, both of them sitting down at the outside tables. Taz dialed Waneka, who was working the drive thru that day.

"Taz, I am at work, what ya want?" She answered.

"It's two people sitting outside ya'll restaurant that I need someone to eavesdrop on. Can you do it?"

Waneka glanced out of the drive thru window and spotted the light skinned girl and the man sitting with her.

"My break is in five minutes, I guess so. What you listening for? Is that one of ya hoes? Is that why I haven't seen you in like two weeks?"

"Look either you can do it or you can't. I got that ass tonite if you do this for me."

She looked again and yelled to her co-worker that she was taking her break right then. "Yeah, I got you boo. You gone let me ride on top this time?"

Taz smiled as he pictured her ass bouncing up and down on him. "Work this out for me shorty and you can ride any way you want." He said.

Giggling she walked out the back door grabbing her cigarettes. She told him to hold on as she walked outside.

Waneka was a ghetto broad Taz met while making a drop off in her hood. That day she happened to be wearing a black halter top and super tight jeans and her curvaceous body caught his attention. The blond weave she was wearing accented her bronzed colored skin. As soon as he had taken her to Red Lobster he was able to hit it that same night. Waneka was a professional dick rider. She worked him every which way but upside down which she was going to try if he hadn't of dropped her on her head. Clearing his head of their sexual episode he paid attention to her as he watched her walk outside to sit next to Taysha and T-money. She was wearing her uniform with her breast exposed at the top. Her hair was up in a ponytail and her make-up was caked on heavy. Her long nails were painted various bright colors of which Taz could see even from across the street. She sat down and pulled out her cigarettes.

"Sounds like this guy is talking about some type of plan. He says it is worth 50 gees. They trying to get revenge on someone." She whispered.

Taz just listened as his anger began to build. He waited to hear more.

Waneka began coughing from the cigarette smoke and cleared her throat catching Taysha's attention. Turning to look at her Taysha rolled her eyes. Waneka just smiled and excused herself.

"Stay focused Waneka, please!" Taz needed to get as much information as he could.

"This girl knows who they are seeking revenge on and she has agreed to do it. Says she doesn't want her name in it or this person will kill her. Sounds like they are friends cause she is starting to cry." Waneka crossed her legs and looked around for Taz's truck.

Taz squinted his eyes to see Taysha wiping tears from her face. He was pissed that Taysha would stoop so low but he knew she was a money hungry hoe.

Waneka spotted the black truck behind another car in front of a white house across the street. Smiling she continued, "This guy is willing to pay her $25,000 if it goes through. Damn I might need to get in on that." Waneka turned to look at T-money knowing he had to have money from the expensive chain around his neck and the diamonds in his ears.

"Look Taz baby, my break is up now so I gotta go."

"Did you catch a name of who they are trying to get?"

"Yeah someone named Trap or Trust or something funny

like that." She stood up and straightened her uniform shirt.

"Alright thanks baby, call me when you get off. I'll try to hook up with you after work."

Smiling Waneka popped the gum in her mouth loudly and put her phone in her pocket. She walked back inside the restaurant.

Hitting the steering wheel Taz's eyes were bloodshot from the weed and his anger mixing together. He wanted to take both of them out in broad daylight but knew that was a bad move with all the witnesses hanging around. T-money was seeking revenge on Truth for shooting him and had planned to involve her best friend, Taysha through the process. Taz was lost in thought when Dub C opened the truck door and got in. He noticed the look on Taz's face.

"Damn dog what the fuck? You look like you on some murder shit."

"I am, it's just a matter of time. It's about to be a mutha-fucking war out here ma nigga."

"Straight up? Well tell me where I fit in cause ya know a nigga like me been looking for a reason to pop my tech."

"All in due time....all in due time." He started his truck and made a u-turn skirting the other way.

After agreeing to the deal Taysha jumped back in her car and headed off home making sure she hadn't been seen by anyone. She was shaking from being so nervous around T-money. The fact he was so calm around her made her even more nervous. She had planned to take the money from the deal and move to Seattle to live with her aunt. There was no way if the plan went down successfully she would live to see another day.

TJ was sitting on his porch when Taz pulled up in his truck and stopped abruptly. Trigger and Truth had left twenty minutes prior to his arrival. Truth was going to drive him to his garage so he could get one of his cars. TJ knew Taz was on something as soon as he jumped out. He noticed sitting in the truck was five of the cities worst criminals. Jap, Pun B, Marky and Kicker were all felons who had been incarcerated a time or two for various crimes. They were grimey niggas who loved the smell of trouble. TJ closed the front door so that Shaquena would not come out.

"Damn what's this? You got the crew and shit, what you on bruh?" TJ looked from Taz to all of the men sitting in the truck.

"Man it's some shit about to go down tonight, get in the truck we'll talk on the way."

TJ obeyed and jumped in the front seat. On the way to his house Taz told him all about the meeting T-money had with Taysha and what Waneka had overheard. They put their own plan into action.

● ● ●

After truth dropped her father off at his car she got a phone call on her cell phone from Taysha.

"Hey girl let's go to the mall, I need some shoes."

"Damn Tay you got enough to start your own shoe store, why you need more?"

"There is a party in the Hills tonight and I got us passes to go."

"Word? The Hills? Damn, is it a superstar or what?"

Taysha thought of the best lie she could think of. "Yeah girl you know Usher and them gone be there, Ludicrous, Missy, all of 'em. They are having some event to raise money for that disaster that happened in New Orleans."

Truth mulled it over for a minute. "Tay, you my girl and all, but who you fuck to get invited to that?"

Taysha laughed nervously.

"You know me I always fuck wit' them paid niggas. Just ran across the right one at the right time. But for real Truth you down or what cause the shit starts at 7 and its 6:15 now."

"Damn, talk about last minute. Ok bitch, come get me from my momma house."

Taysha twiddled her fingers. The plan called for her to get Truth away from her families' vicinity. Trying to think fast she thought of the perfect location. "Naw girl you know yo mom's too nosey for me. Meet me at the Ruckers Bar out near the expressway, we gon go in a Limo."

"Damn, a limo too? That's far as fuck, it'll take me 20 minutes to get there."

"Truth, damn, you got a new truck, aint like you gon waste gas, plus that way we will be like ten minutes away from the party."

Truth thought about it and knew that Taysha was right. The Hills was an exclusive club that was invitation only and you had to be somebody or with someone who was somebody to get in.

"Fine, I'll meet ya there. I thought you wanted to go to the mall though?"

"Yea well I'll just go and meet ya, that way, we get there on time."

"Alright, that sounds like a winner, see you then."

She hung up with Taysha and realized she left her phone charger at home for her cell phone. The low battery indicator was beginning to make a ringing noise so she turned her cell off. Taysha looked over at T-money and nodded her head with tears in her eyes to let him know the plan was a go.

Taz kept dialing Truth's cell phone but kept getting her voicemail. He began to worry.

TJ had called Shaquena to let her know he was out with his brother and to stay by the phone.

"I can't reach her dog." Taz looked over at TJ.

They were sitting outside of her mother's house.

"Damn, we gon have to go to the door and ask Legacy if she checked in." TJ said.

"If we alert Legacy to anything she'll call Trigger, you know that and if he get involved, man, it's gon be some shit." Taz said as he took a sip from the bottle of Hennessy in his lap.

"Nigga, this our fucking sister, if she in trouble we gotta have her back. If something happen to her and Trigger finds out we knew and didn't tell him he gon kill us anyway." TJ wanted too badly to hurt someone for all the pent up frustration he was feeling.

They sat there in the truck trying to decide whether or not to alert Legacy to what was going on. Tired of just sitting around TJ jumped out and ran to the door. Taz jumped out behind him.

"What the hell man, we didn't agree to this!"

"Fuck you, if we sit on our ass our sister could be dead, I'm going to see what Legacy knows."

He ran up to the porch and started banging on the door. Dressed in a silk robe with her hair tied up, Legacy opened the door.

"Well damn, what the hell both of ya'll doing here. Must be a family reunion. Where my baby at?" She looked from Taz to TJ and to the truck full of men in front of her house.

"Somethings wrong, I can feel it. Where is Truth?" Legacy asked again.

Both stood there silent. As if on cue, Trigger appeared from behind the door catching TJ and Taz off guard. They looked at each other and then to their father.

"What's going on? You two are never in the same place at once unless its some bullshit, so kick it to me. Where is your sister?" Trigger asked

TJ started speaking first, he didn't want Trigger involved at all but he knew there was no turning back now.

• • •

On the South Side of town

Assault was nodding his head to his favorite song by Tupac *Only God Can Judge Me*, Sitting in his truck, he waited for T-money to pull up. He thought about the plan they had put together to kidnap Trigger's only girl and just hoped it went through. T-money and Assault were cousins and had found out Truth was talking to both of them when T-money was telling him about the attempted robbery. Pulling up in his truck, T-money dressed in all black, jumped out and walked over to Assault's vehicle.

"Ma nigga, open this door so we can get this shit to crackin,'" T-money was ready to get the plan in motion.

"So what's the deal?"

"She thinks she's going to an industry party. I got it set up for Daron to drive the limo and take her to the spot up in the mountains. Once we get her there we gon contact her father through her brother Taz. I got his number and if he don't cooperate, we already got that plan in action. They all gon feel it."

Assault contemplated the plan. He knew T-money had tendency to get over excited about things and would end up messing up. "I'll do you one better, we gon get her in the limo and what not and drive her over to Lalah's hideaway out in Bakersfield. Once she's there she can't escape. Then we just play the waiting game to see if he will come through." Assault said.

They sat in the truck going over the details of the kidnapping.

• • •

While Truth was getting ready for the party at Taysha's house she noticed that Taysha was unusually quiet. They had changed the plan to get dressed together instead of meeting up. Taysha was trying to buy time so she rearranged the meeting spot without telling T-money what she did. She knew Truth would grow suspicious and either leave or call her brothers if she didn't see Taysha at the meeting spot. Truth watched her friend sitting deep in thought.

"Um, Tay, you ok girl? You been acting funny all night."

Taysha looked up at her friend. She felt horrible about what she was about to put her best friend through. They had been friends since they were ten years old. Faking a smile, Taysha stood up. "Girl, I'm fine, just been tired lately is all."

Her cell phone was ringing. It was T-money calling her. She was supposed to meet him so she could get the exact details of what to do and where to go. She didn't answer the call as she started to change her mind. Thinking of how much Truth was there for her even when her mother died, she felt regret at even thinking of setting her up.

T-money rang her cell phone again. This time she answered it and left the room so Truth couldn't overhear.

"Yeah,"

"Tay, don't get weak on me. It's too much at stake for you to turn back now."

"She is my best friend. I can't do this to her. She's been through enough already."

"See…..," he paused trying to calm his anger.

"Look, if you don't get her to the location in 20 minutes, you will die, it's just that simple," he hung up the line on her.

Taysha looked around and searched for the picture of her mother. She pulled the photograph out of its frame and placed it inside of her bra. "If I don't make it, I'll be seeing you mommy," she said quietly.

Truth walked in the room wearing a small black skirt with three inch stilettos and a sequined black halter top. Her hair was braided on one side and the rest was left to hang down on her shoulder. She looked like something out of a fashion magazine. She smiled because she was excited and ready to go.

Taysha had on a black two piece suit with no bra and one button holding the jacket closed. Slipping on her shoes she avoided eye contact with Truth. They walked out the door where there was a black stretch limo sitting out front waiting on them. Truth was overly excited and ran to the Limo as a man dressed in all black got out and opened the door. Taysha hesistated before climbing in the back with her. She knew the driver was one of T-money's boys. He winked at her as she was getting in. The limo pulled off, headed to the secluded place T-money had chosen. In the limo both girls were quiet. Truth had drifted off in her own thoughts. She thought about her parents and her brothers and how thankful she was that she had all of them. Taysha was shaking inside and tried to keep her palms from sweating. When the limo stopped, both girls sat straight up. Truth frowned. The building she was expecting was not the Hills elite club, it was more of a hole in the wall. There were two men dressed in black who approached the vehicle. One of them opened the door and covered his face. He reached out for Truth's hand but she was apprehensive.

"Taysha, what the fuck is this?"

Taysha looked at her friend and began to cry. "I'm sorry

Truth," was the last word she heard Taysha say before she was hit in the head with a heavy object. The two men dragged her out of the car, the two men picked her up and carried her up the hill to the house where they would hold her hostage. Taysha was crying uncontrollably in the limo when she heard footsteps approach her. Looking in on her, Assault cocked his head to the side.

"You must be Taysha. Just wanted to say thanks fo' looking out for a brotha."

He climbed in the limo and closed the door. Pulling his penis out of his pants he grabbed her hand and pulled her closer. Taysha was scared and began shaking.

"Please don't," she pleaded

"Fuck you bitch. You don't even give a damn about yo' friend, so get over here and give me that shit I been hearing so much about." Assault tapped the window, the driver pulled out a condom and passed it to him.

"Gotta strap up with a hoe like you."

Taysha tried to go for the door only to be pulled back by her hair. She screamed in pain and fell back against the seat.

"You ain't getting' out of this. What did you think, we were just gon let ya ass go?" he looked at her and smiled showing his dimples.

The door opened and T-money rubbed his hands together. "We got her tied up and shit." Looking over at Assault with his pants open, he looked at Taysha.

"Damn whats going on in here, looks like I interrupted something." He stared at Taysha.

Tears was running down her face mixing with her makeup. She remained silent out of fear.

"She's giving out free pussy, come get some. Oh, but you gotta strap up." Assault was sliding the condom on his erection.

T-money knew Assault was lying from the look on Taysha's face. Shaking his head, he backed up out of the limo and shut the door leaving the two alone. Taysha knew she was in for it when the front window was rolled up to give them even more privacy. Assault pulled his jacket off and got on top of her. Taysha started to kick and scream and kicked her heel into his thigh. This angered him and Assault slapped her as hard as he could. Trying her best to fight back she punched and hit him. With his erect penis in his hand, he forced her legs open and shoved himself inside of her. Even with all of her struggle she was no match for his strength and she tired out. She cried as he pushed into her harder and harder as if he were trying to break her back. He grabbed her head and dug his nails in the back of her neck as he reached a climax. Climbing off of her, he pulled the condom off, rolled the window down and threw it outside. With no remorse for what he had done he pulled the pistol out of his waist band and shot Taysha in the head, killing her. He watched her body slump on the seat as the blood poured all over her black suit. He exited the limo and shook his head.

"Damn shame, a bitch like that had to go to waste. She was fine too. If she had cooperated, her pussy would've been the shit." He told the driver. Assault grabbed a towel from his truck and wiped the blood from his face.

T-money looked inside the limo and had to turn his back so he wouldn't see Taysha's face. They had already discussed that they would kill her and split the money in half.

"Time to make that call ma nigga," Assault tapped T-money on the shoulder and handed him the cell phone. T-money felt Assault was getting too far in by his actions and had never seen his cousin acting like that. He wondered if they were even going about the whole situation the right way. T-Money walked out of the room to make the call and he by passed the room

Truth was being held in. He watched as she slept peacefully. For a brief second, he actually felt bad and wanted to let her go. She was young and still had her whole life ahead of her to do what she wanted. Assault caught T-money just standing by the doorway of the room staring at Truth.

"Nigga damn, is you gon fantasize or make the call? We need that money."

T-money snapped out of his daydream and walked down the hall towards the basement to make the call. He didn't want Assault to see how nervous he really was. This was the first time in his life when he was actually doubtful about the outcome.

CHAPTER TEN

WHEN IT GETS GANGSTA!!!!

Taz sat in Legacy's living room staring at his father. When they showed up looking for Truth they didn't expect their father to be at the house. Trying not to alert him to trouble was hard because Trigger was good at reading people. TJ was sitting in a chair trying to avoid eye contact. He had his own thoughts going on.

"I'm gonna ask ya'll both one more time, what the fuck is going on with my baby girl that you came over here to ask Cy if she seen her?"

Legacy was pacing the floor. She became worried when she had tried to dial Truth's cell phone but kept getting her voicemail.

All of them were quiet until there was a pounding at the door. Trig answered the door, it was Jap, who had been sitting in the truck. He had Taz's phone in his hand. He placed his finger to his lips to shush everyone and then he handed the phone to Taz and hit the speakerphone button.

"Speak it," Taz said calmly

"Taz my man, what's good. This ya boy. I got a deal for ya I am sure you might be interested in." T-money said.

Taz swallowed and wondered what T-money was on. He knew he wasn't calling him about a drug deal.

"Ok, shoot it to me."

"Straight up? Ok...Ok.... well see, I got this problem and well, it's your problem too."

Trigger narrowed his eyes. The feeling he had in his stomach was not a good one at all.

"Word? Sounds like you talking about a bitch." Taz knew T-money was still mad about him fucking his girl, Aquanetta a month earlier. He figured he was trying to hook up with Truth as payback until she had him set up.

Laughing, T-money said, "It's a bitch alright, she's not yours though. See ma nigga, she belongs to me now until she is financially paid for."

TJ, Trigger and Legacy listened intently.

"Who you talkin' 'bout?" Taz asked. Taz held the phone so hard he could have crushed it if it were made of glass.

After a slight pause T-money revealed who he was talking about. "That fine ass sister of yours. Yeah, see, we got her little ass all nice, comfy and cozy. And until you come up with $100,000, she belongs to me."

T-money started laughing.

Trigger was upset and slammed his fist into the wall. TJ's eyes were bloodshot red from anger. Taz was trying to remain calm but beads of sweat were forming on his forehead and he was shaking from his own anger taking over. Legacy fell to her knees and began weeping.

"Check this here, if you so much as lay a finger on my baby sister I will have your fucking head." Taz yelled into the phone.

"Nigga, fuck yo lame ass threats. Get my money or she dies, its just that simple. You a nigga from the streets, you know the deal, this is business, never personal. I'll be calling back." He hung up.

Trigger was already in gear when he picked up his phone and started dialing up his crew. Taz didn't want his father's anger to get Truth killed so he was going to try to calm him down but Legacy got to him first.

"Look Trig, I think we need to get the police in on this, ya'll gon go out there and one of you might not come back." She looked at TJ and Taz who were expressing the same emotions Trigger was. Not wanting to say it but knowing she had to try so she said, "Tasty would not want her boys out here like that." Legacy looked at all three of them. They all just stared at her. She had caught their attention.

"Man fuck that, my baby sister has been kidnapped by some asshole who thinks he gon get away with this shit. If I die tryin' to get her back then so be it." TJ was standing up.

Legacy was crying and trying to calm everyone down but it became too much.

Trigger had called all the people he knew that were on his team to come by. Taz was outside alerting Jap and the rest of the crew of the phone call. A war was getting ready to take place and there was no turning back. As Legacy sat in the corner of the room in a chair, she watched several men come in and out of her house. All of them were armed with guns so big that she thought they were going to the army. Trigger's anger was getting the best of him.

"Leave no one alive. I mean it, babies, mothers, aunties, uncles, cousins, they all fucking die. I said and will continue to say until I die, no one fucks wit' ma baby girl." He put the clip in his gun and took a pull from a joint that was passed to him.

TJ was on the phone with a very concerned Shaquena. "Look don't question me right now, its some shit going down and I need to handle it, so just get ya shit and the baby and go to yo fucking momma house in Seattle."

"Damn it TJ, I don't have money to just hop on a plane."
She was concerned at his sudden need for her to leave.

He was getting frustrated with her. "Shaquena, look outside,
there should be a taxi out front."

She opened the curtain and noticed a taxi with two people
in it.

"Inside that taxi will be my guy Rip and his girl Daisy.
They're going to the airport. You're riding the plane with
them, they have your ticket already. Please just get out of LA
and take my son with you."

"TJ, I know we been through our shit but through it all, I
love you baby."

Shaquena had no idea what was going on but knew in her
heart it couldn't be good.

Choking on his emotions, TJ swallowed hard. He prayed
that nothing happened to him where he would never be able
to see his son or his woman again. "I love you too. Kiss Lil T
for me and tell him his daddy loves him. Hurry up and get
outta there and don't stop for nothing."

Quena could not convince TJ to tell her what was going
on so she obeyed his orders, packed her stuff and put the baby's
clothes in a suitcase. Shaquena knew it had to be serious if TJ
was making her leave town. Crying, she left the house with
her baby on her hip and got into the taxi.

Trigger instructed his boys to move the people they loved
out of harms way by sending them away. Taz was glad Ebony
was out of state in Ohio. When he phoned her he planned to
tell her he loved her. She answered the phone on the fourth
ring just as he was getting ready to hang up.

"Yeah, this Ebony,"

"Ebony, I love you," He said.

She paused for a long time. "Taz, what's wrong. You talking to me like you finna die." Ebony was scared.

"They got my baby sister man, shit finna get ill right now. Just know that I love you and I gotta go." Taz was trying to maintain his composure.

Ebony was scared, she knew she had to say what she had been trying to tell Taz for 5 years. She just blurted it out.

"I didn't abort the baby. His name is Tyreek. He's 5." Taz dropped his gun causing it to go off. The bullet shot through the window and shattered in Legacy's living room. Everyone ducked, Legacy screamed and hit the floor.

"Fuck Taz, what's the deal nigga?" Jap asked.

"I'm sorry man, it was an accident."

"Look, get off the phone and let's do this for you kill us all." Trigger said

"Uh Ebony ......why after all this time?...look.....we gon talk later, I gotta go."

"I love you too and I never stopped." She slipped in quickly.

He hung up the phone feeling worse than he felt before he called her. After 5 years of thinking he had lost her to someone else she had been keeping a secret from him all along. He glanced over at Trigger who was staring him down.

"You cool?" Trigger asked

"I'm a father. He 5. Name's Tyreek." He said

"Damn, I'm a grandfather again? Ya'll two niggas I swear gone make me old before my time." Trigger shook his head.

"Alright the rest of the crew is here." Jap yelled out.

Legacy got up to look out her window. Her block looked like a swarm of FBI trucks and cars. There were at least 20 cars and trucks all black in color with dark tinted windows. Tapping her on her shoulder Trigger turned Legacy around.

"I want to ask you to leave if you can. I don't want you

around this bullshit. They gone pull out all stops if we don't give them that money. I will get her back, don't you worry about that. Here are the keys to a house no one knows about, it's in Santa Monica, go there, chill, stay by the phone, I'll call you. There is a girl there, her name is Trudy, she knows the deal so don't sweat her." He handed the keys to her.

Legacy looked at him like he was crazy.

"I wish I would let a muthafucka make me leave when my baby is out here in some other muthafucka's custody over some fucking money. You must be out your rabbit ass mind to think I'm leaving. You been playing superman for so long doing everything for her, pushing me to the background. Let me tell you something nigga, it was my legs she slid out of and my body she set up camp in for 9 months. It was me reading and bathing her ass when you was out in them streets. ME! I am her mother and no one, not even you, can take that away from me. So if you don't mind, I'll stay right the fuck here and wait." She crossed her arms across her chest.

Legacy was sick of being told what to do when it came to Truth and took a stand on it.

Trigger just looked at her. He knew Legacy wouldn't leave but he had to try anyway. He passed her a shotgun.

"Kill anything that moves and tries to come in on you, don't talk and don't listen. No words can be said right now until Truth is brought home."

He kissed her on the lips and walked out the door.

In separate vehicles Trigger, Taz, TJ and the rest of the men were prepared to kill and take down anything and anyone who was associated with T-money. Taz had enough information on him that he knew all of his whereabouts and all of his stash spots. One of his girls, Zaria, used to fuck with both of them at the same time but liked Taz more. She leaked all of T-money's information to him one night while they were drunk and high and Taz made note of everything she said knowing one day it would come in handy. The first stop they made would be to his grandmother's house.

Up in the Hills

T-money was pacing the floor. Assault was watching TV in the front room of the place they were in. It was a cabin that mostly hunters and newlyweds rented to get away from the rest of the city. Hidden by trees and set high atop the mountains it was not easy to locate. After killing Taysha, Assault had his guy dump the limo and the body in the river.

Truth was tied to a bed in the small bedroom when she started to regain consciousness.

"Damn nigga, don't you think you gave them enough time, call that ass back." Assault said. He wanted to get this shit over with as soon as possible. What he didn't know was the power Trigger held on most of the hood niggas in LA.

T-money picked up the phone and forgot to block out his cell number. Dialing Taz again, he picked up on the first ring. "What up ma nigga, you got that paper?"

Taz blew the smoke out of his mouth and took a swig from his Hennessy bottle.

"Naw, you know it's gon' be a minute before I cop that, man. I ain't balling like that no more."

They both knew it was a lie. With all of the money Taz mother left him and all the money he made in the streets, he had well over 3 million dollars saved up. He was killing time as they made their rounds threatening all of T-money's people to give up any information on his whereabouts. They were outside of his grandmother's house when T-Money had called.

"Well I'm gon' tell you. You got until 6am to get me the

fucking money our ya baby sister will have gun powder pumped in her."

Taz just smiled as he watched T-money's grandmother outside in her yard. "Kill that noise, we'll have your money, and I'm gon' keep telling you, if you so much as lay a hand on my sister, you will regret it."

T-money laughed.

Keeping it real to his word, Taz jumped out of the truck, ran up to T-money's grandmother and put a gun to her temple. She struggled to move but stopped when he put his arm around her neck and pulled it in close choking her. Holding his phone with his free hand he said, "Listen to this muthafucka, if my sister is touched you will lose the one bitch whose always had your back."

T-money listened to what sounded like his grandmother in the background as she sounded like she must have been choking. He knew he was in over his head with things when he realized they were not going to just hand over the money with ease. Trig and weem're playing hard ball and if he showed any sign of weakness they would win.

"Ok, check it ..." he walked out the room so Assault wouldn't hear him.

"Don't hurt my grandmom's, she innocent man, just get me the money and Truth goes untouched."

"Yeah, you betta hope that's true ma nigga, or else it's gon' be a lot of funerals in LA because of you."

Taz pushed her back in the house leaving two of his boys Marky and Kicker with her. They were to sit by the phone and wait for the signal to let her live or die.

Taz jumped back in the truck and sped off. He dialed both TJ and Trigger's phones to let them know what T-money had said.

Assault was tired of waiting. He knew kidnapping the daughter of the worst criminal next to him was going to be difficult. He went to the room to check on her. Even though he had her tied up and gagged he thought she was still beautiful with her mini skirt and sequined top. She looked up and her eyes grew wide. She was sure she wasn't going to make it out alive. Tears started streaming down her face again. Assault rubbed her face with his hand. "Aww pretty girl, don't cry. It will all be over before you know it. As long as your daddy cooperates, we all good."

Truth watched him as he got up and paced the small bedroom. She noticed Assault had blood on his shoes and his pants and immediately her thoughts went to Taysha. She remembered that no one had grabbed her before she was knocked unconscious. As if he were reading her mind, he answered the question she wanted to know.

"Oh, by the way, your hoe ass friend Taysha, she got some good pussy." He smelled his fingers.

Truth turned her head and tried to keep from throwing up.

"If she hadn't of betrayed you, I would have let her live. See your girl was the one that set all this up. She got us to you. All we had to do was pay her."

Truth was shaking her head and crying, she couldn't believe what Assault was telling her.

He nodded back. "Yes she did it. I know its crazy right? Sometimes that shit make you wanna kill. Yeah your father knows about betrayal real well." Assault took a swig from the bottle of Vodka he had in his hand.

Truth stared at him. He continued to talk.

"Yeah your daddy betrayed me back when we were 16 years old. You had just been born I believe. He and I had pulled the biggest hustle there was. We robbed this nigga named Gabriel who went by the name G-funk. The night your momma was in labor with you as a matter of fact was the night we pulled that shit off and still got her to the hospital in time to have you. I was only 14 at the time."

Assault stopped, he felt like he was revealing too much but he hadn't told any one why his anger and hatred for Trigger was so great and since he had been drinking all night the liquor was making him tell the truth.

Truth wanted him to finish. She needed to know what the deal was between Assualt and her father. It would explain why Assault hated Trigger. If only she knew what the beef between them was all about.

T-money walked in the room and saw Assault standing by Truth. He heard him talking to her and came to see what the conversation was about.

"Man, what the fuck you doing?" He asked. He noticed the bottle of Vodka that Assault was holding on to.

"I was talking to her," Assault looked at T-money.

"Fuck a talk, we gotta stay focused. These niggas playing dirty man. They got Grandma Joe in this mess. It's niggas camped out at the fucking crib and shit."

"How do you know?" Assault asked.

"I called the crib and a muthafucka answered talking about she can't come to the phone. When you ever known Grandma not to want to be on the phone."

Assault looked at Truth and his anger was starting to rise all over again. His grandmother was important to him and he didn't want his bullshit to get her killed so his moma could hate him more than she already did.

"Man fuck, how the hell they know where she lived?"

They both turned to Truth and looked at her.

She was scared as they approached her.

"Did you send your daddy to my grandmom's house?" Assault asked. He pulled his pistol out and rubbed her thigh.

Crying again she just shook her head.

T-money pulled Assault up out of Truth's face. He didn't trust Assault, drunk or sober when he had a pistol in his hand. He saw him take too many lives without remorse and didn't want to chance him shooting Truth.

"Look, they said if we hurt her they gon' kill Grandmom's, so chill nigga, aight?" T-money put Trigger's hand on his shoulder to move him back.

Assault looked at him like he was crazy.

"Nigga, a lot of bodies gon' drop. If Grandma gotta die over this shit then so be it. I'm gon' kill that nigga." He pulled a small blue pill out of his pocket and swallowed it.

"Don't get to popping no ecstacy pills nigga, what the fuck." T-money was concerned that his cousin was out of control.

Assault wasn't concerned about anything or anyone.

"Man they gon' have me right, cause if I think about the shit too much I'm not gone do it." Assault replied, he sat down on the bed and licked Truth's neck.

"Man they said don't hurt her right? Well what if we fuck her?" Assault asked.

"Damn nigga, you fucking up. How much pussy you need? You raped her friend and killed her, how you gon' come in here and fuck *her* after that? Yo man, you on that bullshit and you need to get back on track." T-money was concerned that the situation was getting out of hand.

Grabbing the bottle of Vodka from Assault, he left the room.

At the news of her friends death Truth wanted to cry but she decided to hold back the tears and watch Assault's every move. He stopped feeling her up and got up. His anger was being fueled by the alcohol and the pill he took. He began talking again, this time not even really talking to Truth. His conversation was more to the air because that was where he was looking .

"That muthafucka took off with over $100,000 in his possession. The police were everywhere. After I pumped six shots in a cop I was hit by a car and broke my leg. We were supposed to work together but he took off in the opposite direction. I had to serve time for that nigga and I didn't get one fucking penny. Bitch ass nigga didn't even put nothing on my books or nothing. He left me hanging. And there was no love when I got out. All I heard was he was the man on the streets. The head nigga in charge and shit."

He looked at Truth. She was staring at him. She figured he was talking again about her father. She now understood what the beef was. Assault felt like her father played him and let him serve time for something they did together. Her back was sore and her stomach was in pain from not eating. She couldn't believe after almost 18 years that Assault was still holding on to that drama. Truth looked over at Assault who was staring off into space like he was lost in thought. It bothered Truth. She knew Assault was dangerous and could kill her at anytime. She sincerely hoped her brothers and her father would be able to reach her before it was too late.

CHAPTER ELEVEN

'TIL DEATH DO US PART

Sitting in his truck high from smoking a blunt, Trigger was trying to analyze the situation. He had known T-money for awhile and knew he could not have devised a plan to kidnap his daughter alone. He sat in thought trying to figure out who the real mastermind could be behind the whole operation. Him and his crew were parked outside of T-money's ex-girl-friend, Zaria's house. He planned on asking her all she knew about T-money's connections and the people he hung with the most. He knew his son had messed around with her a few times and he decided to use him to get information out of her. On his phone he made the call to Taz who was in the truck behind him.

"So, you gon' go in there and if you gotta eat the bitch pussy, get her to call that nigga and let her come to him. Knowing how stupid T-money is, when it comes to women he'll be sloppy and think nothing of it." Trigger was for sure that his plan would work.

The crew had been circling blocks for almost two hours and were coming up with nothing from any of the people they knew on the streets. They even tried to ride down on T-Money baby momma's but both women stuck to stories of not hearing from him.

"Man Trig, I don't know, he might catch on. Zaria ain't exactly on good terms with him. He knows she fucked wit' me before." Taz was unsure of the plan Trigger had in mind.

"Well do something to convince her to get to him or at least find out. It's already 11. I swear if ma baby girl dies I will hold everyone responsible."

Taz felt Trigger's frustration. They were getting nowhere and time was passing. He got out of his truck. He noticed TJ jumped out behind him.

"What you doing man?" Taz asked TJ.

"Look, you don't know what shit this bitch could be on so I'm gonna have ya back," TJ said.

They walked up to her apartment building and rang the buzzer. With a sleepy voice, Zaria asked who was at her door. After telling her who it was she buzzed them in.

Walking to her door they smelled incense burning. Zaria appeared at the door wearing a silk robe. She held it together with her hand exposing the top portion of her voluptuous breasts.

"Well Taz, long time no see. Come in." She held the door open and purposely blocked the small doorway with her frame so that they would have to rub up against her to get by. Entering the small apartment the brothers were apprehensive about moving further into the dark, living room. TJ made sure he had his back towards a wall in case someone was in the room. There was movement from the back bedroom. Taz and TJ looked at Zaria.

"You got company?" TJ asked.

Smiling she flipped on the kitchen light to illuminate the hallway they were standing in. "Yea, but if you got something for me I can get rid of him." She eyed the bulge in TJ's jeans. He was aroused at her appearance but would never take the chance with a hoe like her. Taz was growing impatient. He couldn't ask her what he needed to ask her until he found out who it was in her bedroom.

"TJ, stay here with Zaria while I check her bedroom. Are you sure it's just one person here?"

She turned her attention away from TJ and looked at Taz putting her hands on her hips. "What you think, I'm some kind of hoe? I said it's a nigga in my bed and that's it."

Taz knew better. Zaria's history and track record with men included her letting men fuck her for money, sometimes letting two or three hit it back to back. He pulled the pistol he was carrying from his waistband.

"Look Taz, don't come up in this muthafucka tripp'n. I gotta live here." She said growing nervous at the sight of his gun.

"I'm not on drama. If everything is like you say it is then it should be cool. TJ, hold it down in here." Taz slid along the wall and walked into the small bedroom. Lying in the bed asleep was a naked woman of petite stature. Next to her was a white man who was fully dressed and sweating.

Throwing up his hands he said, "Look man, I don't want no trouble. I just met her last night and I paid her to suck my dick. Then she and her girlfriend asked if I would do a three-some for $200 and I agreed. My money is in my pocket and my name is Chester."

Chester was sweating profusely. Taz just shook his head and opened up the closet to make sure no one else was in the room. Checking under the bed he confirmed that the only two in the room was the guy named, Chester and the sleeping girl. He looked the man in the eye.

"Chester, is it? You didn't see or hear nothing right?" Taz

grabbed his wallet that he was holding in Chester's hand. Pulling out his license he read the address.

"21354 Cherrylawn Dr., Chester Sykowski. I'll be keeping this just to be sure we got an understanding."

Chester nodded his head fearing for his life.

Walking back down the hallway Taz heard the bathroom door creak. He immediately turned around and Zaria tried to intervene.

"See, I told you no one else was in here, where are you going?" She tried to walk down the hallway but TJ grabbed her. He knew something was up when Taz turned around.

Kicking the door to the bathroom, the door hit the bath tub. Flipping the switch on, Taz aimed his gun and pulled back the shower curtain. Standing there in the shower was one of T-money's boys, Kayoz. He was holding on to his pants trying to pull them up. Taz just shook his head as he remembered one of the things Trigger always taught them. Never get caught with your pants down. He aimed his pistol at dude's head.

"Don't make no sudden moves and I'll let you live." Taz watched as he stepped out of the bathtub slowly. Kayoz looked over by the toilet at his gun sitting on top of it. Following his eye Taz watched him.

"If you think about reaching for that gun, I will splatter your brains all over this bathroom."

Taz guided Kayoz out and down the hallway. TJ had Zaria pinned up against the wall. Her eyes grew big when she saw Taz walking all three people down the hallway to the living room. He had awakened the sleeping girl and made Chester get up. All of them were held at gunpoint.

"Don't nobody move or you will all die. Try nothing and you will all live." Taz said. He directed the hostages to sit on the couch.

He threw the naked girl a blanket from the chair so that she could cover herself.

"This some bullshit Taz, and you know it."

He looked at Zaria being held by his brother and just smiled.

Chester continued sweating profusely. Kayoz was staring at both men.

"What do you know about T-money's plan to kidnap my sister?" Taz asked.

"Man, I don't know shit." Kayoz lied, he was one of the people T-money contacted after he found out Taz had sent men to his grandmother's house.

Knowing he was lying Taz tried it again. "One mo' time, I'm gon' ask you. What the fuck do you know about my sister's whereabouts? I know he told you where he is and I need to know."

Kayoz hated TJ and Taz with a passion. He felt they were spoiled because of their father. He grew up in a foster home and never knew what family life was like and resented others who did. "Man fuck you, I ain't saying shit."

Taz and TJ both aimed their guns at him. TJ still had Zaria pinned and was still able to aim his gun at Kayoz. Chester tried to move out of range but Taz shot him in the chest. His body slumped over on the couch as he bled.

"I said don't no one fucking move." Taz was getting impatient.

Chester struggled to breathe as more blood spilled from his chest.

Zaria was struggling with TJ to no avail. Her petite frame against his was no match. He overpowered her and pushed her to the living room with the others. She watched Chester bleed and felt sorry for him. Earlier he had told her he was married and his wife had cancer and couldn't please him anymore.

Sitting next to the other girl they embraced each other. Kayoz was unmoved. Death had become a normal spectator event in his life. He was mad at himself for losing his piece.

"I'm gon' ask you again, where the fuck is T-money holding my sister at?"

"I'm gon' tell you again, I ain't telling you shit," Kayoz was glaring at them. TJ hit him in the head with the back of his gun causing both women to jump.

Laughing from frustration Taz was shaking his head. He watched Kayoz struggle with the pain the blow caused.

"Ok, I see you want this to be easy. You just want us to kill you and that'll be it so you don't go out like no snitch. Naw, I'm not gon' let it be that easy for you." He moved closer to him looking him dead in the eye.

"This my sister we talking about, my blood. You betta start singing or that pretty little ass girl of yours is gonna be in a body bag. Yeah, I know ya baby momma, Monica. We go wayyy back." Taz was lying. He never even met her but he knew her name through other people. He also knew Kayoz had a baby by her.

This caught Kayoz's attention. His daughter was only a year old and was the only happiness he had in his messed up life. He knew he would die either way if he did or didn't tell.

"Look man, don't harm my daughter. I'll tell you what you want to know." Kayoz knew he was signing his own death certificate on both sides. He said a silent prayer for his daughter before he told them what they wanted to know.

Taz eased up and pulled back the gun.

"He got her at some Hunter's lodge up in the mountains. I'm supposed to meet him there to transport her to another location if ya'll didn't come through with the money by the time he gave you."

"What time?"

"12,"

Taz and TJ looked at their watches. It was 11:30.

"Is he alone?" Taz asked

Kayoz hesistated, he was not supposed to reveal Assault's dealings in it at all ,but he figured since they would kill him anyway he might as well go all out.

Sighing loudly he continued, "NO. Assault and several other men are with him. They got guards on watch."

Hearing the name Assault alerted both TJ and Taz. They knew of the ongoing beef he had with their father.

TJ had a plan.

"Give us the keys to your car."

Taz looked at his brother.

"We gon' let you live long enough to get us to that location. You already a walking dead man. If we don't kill you they will, but we need to know you telling the truth." TJ said.

They watched Kayoz grab keys from his pants pocket. He handed them over. Zaria just shook her head at Kayoz wondering why he would set himself up like that.

They grabbed Kayoz and let him lead the way. Looking back at Zaria, Taz knew he had to handle her. She was a witness and he knew he couldn't trust her. Locking eyes it was as if Zaria already knew what Taz was thinking.

"If you gon' kill me at least let me get some things off my chest." Tears started rolling down her face.

He shook his head and aimed both of his pistols at her and her girlfriend. Zaria jumped up trying to stop him ,but was stopped short by the bullet to her neck. Her girlfriend took a bullet to the head. Grabbing hold of Kayoz both TJ and Taz fled down the stairs before anyone could notice them. While in the parking garage walking to the car, Taz called his father who had been parked outside.

"Yo Trig, we cool, had 3 witnesses we took care of, but we got one of T-money's boys. He said it's Assault that is behind the whole plan. T-money is just a pawn in the game."

Trigger hit his hand against the steering wheel. He knew someone else had something to do with it. It angered him even more when he found out it was his arch enemy Assault. He knew for years Assault had hired people to take him out, to no avail.

Taz continued while he knew his father would be lost in thought. "We are going to follow him to the location in his car, he is supposed to meet them at 12am. We are in a black, Monte Carlo."

They hung up and Trigger had his men watch for the car coming out of the garage. They got behind it and trailed the black car. After a 20 minute ride everyone grew impatient. Trigger sensed a problem when they reached the foot of the hills. He stopped his entourage and waited at the bottom. Calling TJ on his cell he wanted to alert them.

"TJ, something ain't right about this situation, tell Taz to pull back." Trigger was sure it was a set up.

TJ and Taz were too far up the hill nearing the cabin to turn around. "We can't, we are already here." TJ said.

"I got a bad feeling about this. Anything to do with Assault is never good. Every move we make has to be thought out or it could cost Truth her life." Trigger was getting concerned.

TJ thought about what he said as they approached the cabin. He tapped Taz on the shoulder. "Dad..I mean Trigger says, we should pull back and just off dude until we can get a plan. He feels it's a setup."

"We too close to back up now, it'll will make us look suspicious." Taz was watching Kayoz park the truck near the driveway of one of the cabins.

Trigger felt like all of his children were in danger. His daughter was at the hands of the enemy and his sons were pawns playing right into his trap. He had to think quickly of a plan to keep them unharmed.

"Fuck it! Pull up and then let dude get out, but let him know you will kill him if he so much as wipes his nose or signals with anything." Trigger told TJ on the phone.

TJ ducked down as Kayoz pulled closer to the cabin's driveway. From the backseat he instructed him on what to do letting him know one false move and he would die.

Watching the car creep up, one of T-money's men on watch alerted both T-money and Assault that Kayoz was now there. Looking out the window Assault sensed something funny about the way Kayoz approached the door when he got out of the car.

Something ain't right He thought to himself. Going over to the room where T-money sat watching Truth he let him know Kayoz had arrived.

"That nigga pulled up slow man. You know how he drives. Slow is not his steelo."

"So, what you saying man? He on some bullshit?" T-money pulled his hat down over his forehead. A gesture he only did when he was nervous

"Or he got some bullshit wit' him." Assault rubbed the front of his pants. The pill was working overtime and T-money had to wrestle him off of Truth several times.

Truth sat with her legs underneath her, cramped from being in one position for so long. She urinated on herself out of fear when Assault pulled his gun out and stuck it up her skirt trying to shove it in her. She hoped she smelled bad so he wouldn't touch her, but since Assault was euphoric and horny he went down on her anyway biting her clit and sucking as hard as he could. Wanting him to stop she tried to kick him but he sat on her feet to keep her from moving and continued on. When he tried to have sex with her T-money walked in and stopped him out of jealousy. Both Assault and T-money went to the window to look out at Kayoz. He was moving slow in a zombie like walk. He approached the door and turned the knob. Walking in he said,

"I'm h…here..for the girl." He was trying to mask his nervousness.

They moved Truth from a sitting position and walked her to the front room. She was now blindfolded and couldn't see.

Outside in the car TJ and Taz were waiting patiently. Kayoz told them he was to transport Truth to another location. The plan was to get Truth in the car unharmed and then unleash on Assault and T-money. Taz was never one to follow directions, nor wait for something to go wrong. When Kayoz had gotten out of the car so had he and walked around to the back where he saw two armed men standing at the door. He saw a hole under the porch and crawled under it lying on his stomach. Pulling out his silencer piece he put it on the gun he was carrying and shot both men in the feet. The weight of the one's body made a crashing noise as he fell. The noise outside sent T-money and Assault running for their guns. Kayoz stood still not knowing what was going on. Truth moved to the wall that she felt with her hands. Assault saw the bodies of his guards bleeding on the back porch and knew it was someone out there. He aimed his gun and stepped out on the porch. Taz was still under the porch when he recognized a pair of Timberland boots worn by his brother standing at the entrance to where he lay.

"Who the fuck are you?" Assault asked TJ who had gotten out of the car to look for his brother.

Oh shit, why did he get out of the car? Taz thought as he tried to get a better aim on Assault's position. He knew with both of them out in the open someone was bound to get hurt. When Trigger sensed danger he had approached the armed guards at the bottom of the hill killing them both with a silenced gun. Their bodies just dropped as he and three other armed men ran up the hill. Trigger noticed the black car they had tailed was now empty.

He could hear Assault's voice.

"T, get out here man! It's some bullshit in the game playa." Assault knew he was high and gone off the ex so he needed T-money's help.

TJ froze in his spot when out walked T-money with a rifle in his hand. "What's the problem?"

Laughing Assault said,

"Looks like Trigger done once again put someone up to do his dirty work. The killa part is this muthafucka is his son. Look at him, he got the same build and every thing."

Taz moved his position towards a window located under the porch. He figured if he could get in he could approach them from behind. To his surprise the window popped right open and he crawled in.

"What should we do with him" T-money was now face to face with TJ who was holding his gun at his side. He looked down at the semi automatic weapon and laughed.

"OH, cause you got a gun I'm supposed to be scared?" T-money pulled up his shirt showing his chest.

"Nigga, I been shot befo,' it ain't shit. So a bullet I aint afraid of."

Assault still high, was laughing.

TJ was standing there and raised his gun to T-money's head. "Where the fuck is my sister you bitch ass nigga. Gotta kidnap a girl just to get money cause you cant hustle it up out in the streets and do yo' time like a real nigga. Too busy being this nigga's side kick to really even realize what the fuck you into." TJ was pulling out all stops.

What he said had pissed T-money off so he raised his shotgun. Trigger was approaching from the side witnessing the interaction. He noticed the shotgun held to TJ's head and the gun TJ had held to T-money's head. He motioned for the other two armed men to go to the front and cause a distraction. Doing as they were told , one busted the glass making everyone jump including Taz who was now in the kitchen approaching the living room.

"Man ,now what the fuck was that and where are those lazy ass guards of yours?" Assault said. He pulled his pistol and walked back in the house leaving TJ and T-money face to face. Trigger continued to approach and almost lost his breath when he saw Truth through one of the windows with a blindfold on. Across her mouth was a bandana and she was standing with her back to the wall. He could tell she was scared by the way she kept shaking her leg. *Baby girl, I'm gonna get you out alive if I have to die trying,* he silently said to himself.

Inside Assault was looking for Kayoz who had miraculously disappeared. Taz was holding him in the kitchen waiting for Assault to walk in. Knowing something was wrong Assault walked over to Truth. Bending down he tried to kiss her but she moved her head when she felt his breath on her shoulder. He looked over her shoulder and out the window locking eyes with Trigger. Thinking he was still high he frowned and closed his eyes and looked up again. Nothing was there but the trees.

"Man I'm fucking losing it," He said out loud and grabbed Truth by the arm to lead her back into the bedroom.

Still standing face to face with guns pointed, TJ and T-money stared each other down. Outside the corner of his eye, TJ saw his father creeping up which was why he was unafraid of pulling his gun on T-money. Seeing the red light on T-money's face from his father's infrared beam he was hoping he would be able to hit him or *he* would be a dead man.

"You might as well give it up." T-money said

"Not until my sister is safe." TJ replied.

In a flash of light T-money's body jerked, his head opened up and he fell to the grown. TJ pumped six more shots in his chest which rang out in the air. Trigger ran around next to him on the back steps. Assault had heard the shots and grabbed Truth even harder forcing her to enter the hallway of the cabin. Seeing two men at the front door, Assault shot both of them with his pistol while still holding on to Truth who was screaming through her gag. She couldn't see what was going on but felt like she was in the middle of a war from all the noise of gunfire. Taz was in the kitchen standing in the dark when he saw the figure move. One of T-money's armed men was in the kitchen and had seen him the whole time. Firing a shot in the dark, the man shot Kayoz killing him instantly with a gunshot to his chest. Taz jumped out the way and fired back as more bullets were fired. Assault hearing the commotion from the kitchen ran out the front door still holding Truth tightly.

"I need the fucking car! Damn this shit is going all muthafucking wrong." He yelled into his walkie talkie. Assault didn't know that his men that were supposed to be at the end of the hill with the car were now dead. Four more shots rang out in the house before Taz finally was able to kill the other armed gunman. He caught a bullet to his left knee and couldn't move.

Trigger and TJ were in the house. "Go see if your brother is ok," he pointed to the kitchen. TJ immediately did as he was told. Assault was strong arming Truth as he made her walk down the gravel path of the driveway.

"Aquarius don't you fucking take another step or I'll blow ya head off." Trigger yelled.

Turning around at the sound of his government name Assault looked at Trigger. "Man I swear you are good. No matter what, you seem to have your hand in every fucking thing. Just can't find good help these days. I should have never trusted T-money or Kayoz for that matter." He was making light of the situation.

"Let her go and we can be men and deal with this bullshit one on one. Truth has nothing to do with this." Trigger was trying to control his finger and the urge to just shoot.

Taking off her blindfold Assault was purposely trying to get to Trigger's emotional side. The only way he could do that was through his most beloved child, his baby girl.

Adjusting her eyes to the light Truth blinked. Looking forward she saw her father staring at her. She wanted to run to his arms but felt the coldness of the steel on her back. Crying again she stood there being held by Assault. Trigger's heart was beating rapidly at the sight of the tears running down his daughter's face.

"Now we can handle this civilly or I can kill her and you take a chance of saving her ass and dying anyway."

TJ and Taz were still inside but could hear the conversation.

"Look man this shit is old. 18 years to be exact. Why you can't let this shit die?"

Trigger was at his wit's end. Seeing Truth's tears were tearing him up inside.

Assault's plan worked, he was getting to Trigger's emotional side. He continued to walk backwards holding the gun in Truth's back. "You know the fucking rules, you came wit' no money, you gets no girl, dumb ass. Ain't you about 33 or so? I would have thought you would be a lot smarter. Check it, we gon' leave right and if you don't have the money by the time you were told, Truth is basically gonna need funeral arrangements."

Assualt continued to walk backwards and Trigger felt helpless. He couldn't shoot because Truth's life would be jeopardized. He was caught between a rock and a hard place. He watched Assault continue to walk away when a shadow of a figure behind them caught his attention. He couldn't make out the face but knew it was a woman from the shape of her body.

Screaming as loud as she could Legacy unloaded the clip of the gun she was holding. Assault never saw it coming. He dropped to his knees. Trigger ran over to Truth who didn't turn around to see her mother. Embracing her and picking her up he held on to Truth for dear life. TJ had come to the front of the porch when he heard Legacy scream. He had managed to find something to stop the bleeding from Taz's wound. He watched as she shot Assault down. Legacy was a disheveled mess. She was still in her robe and had on tennis shoes and a t-shirt underneath it. She had grown impatient and tailed TJ when he went to Zaria's house. She made sure not to alert Trigger that she was following them. When she grew tired of waiting to see if they would come down the hill alive she took matters into her own hands. She had grabbed one of the dead guards guns and started carefully up the hill. After seeing the guy's face who was holding Truth she recalled he was the same one who had raped her in New York. When she saw Truth with a gun to her back she snapped and took aim. Her motherly instincts kicked in and she did what she had to do to protect her only child.

"Oh my baby ,my baby," Legacy had run up to where Trigger was holding Truth and embraced her.

TJ had helped Taz up and onto the porch supporting his weight on his shoulder as he hopped along. They witnessed the three of them hugging in the driveway.

"Thank you Jesus for saving my baby," Legacy said to the sky.

"I told you if it took my life I would bring her home." Trigger said.

Truth was just happy to be in both of her parents' arms safe.

As they stood hugging in the middle of the driveway TJ looked up to see Assault's arm raise with his gun. By the time he called out the words "look out", a shot was fired.

"Noooooooooooooooooooooooooooooooooooo," Truth screamed out.

She watched the body of her parent drop to the ground.

"Oh no .no. no. no. no please God no." Truth was on her knees.

She held her mother's head in her lap. Legacy was struggling to breathe. Assault had fired off one more shot before he finally died. The bullet went straight through piercing Legacy's lungs and major arteries. Trigger was trying to hold her up. He ripped off his shirt to stop the bleeding.

"Please Legacy, fight this shit. Oh God why didn't I just marry ya ass and keep you away from this bullshit."

She struggled to talk. "Trig....... ger.....p...pp...pl..ease ....keep ......ou..r....baby.......s..s...safe." Tears rolled down her face as she felt like the breath in her body was closing in on her.

"Shhhhh, don't talk please, don't talk, you gon' be fine." Tears were rolling down Trigger's cheeks.

TJ was on his cell phone dialing 911.

Truth was sobbing as she stroked her mother's hair.

Trying again to say what she had to say Legacy opened her mouth. "In mmy he...art..you ....we... re.... mm.m m.arried..... to..me...'til ....d...d..death...d...d..do us..part." She started gagging on the blood that was now filling her lungs.

Trigger shushed her again but her body began to convulse as she spit up blood. Truth was crying as she held her mother's body helplessly. Soon everything was still as Legacy stopped moving. Taz and TJ were approaching them.

Trigger felt like he was being punished witnessing again another death of someone he loved dearly.

"Legacy damn you. You were always trying to be so strong." He said to her lifeless body.

"Look, the police are on their way, we gone have to leave." Taz said quietly.

Truth was crying as she closed her mother's eyes and kissed her forehead.

"Bye mommy. I love you." She said as she got up to move. She removed her mother's shirt and covered her face with it.

Everyone heard the sirens in the distance and knew it was time to move around. There would be no way to explain all of the bodies surrounding the cabin. Alex, TJ's friend, had pulled up next to the four of them. TJ had called him right after he called for an ambulance. Alex owned a business just down the mountainside so he knew he could get to them quicker. Seeing the massacred bodies he shook his head and took his hat off. TJ helped Taz into the truck along with Truth who was silent. She kept her head down as she was overcome once again with grief and the tears poured down her face.

"Come on Trigger we gotta go." TJ pleaded. His emotions were building up and he needed to leave the situation. Seeing his baby sister lose her mother right before her eyes was hard for him to deal with and had him reminiscing over his own mother.

Trigger continued to hold on to Legacy's hand.

"I killed both of them. All they wanted was to be with me and I killed both of them. I killed them." Trigger was still sitting next to Legacy's dead body.

Looking at his friend TJ knew he had to make a decision. "Dad, come on it wasn't your fault. Momma used to tell me you can't help who you love."

The sirens were coming closer.

"We gotta go!"

Trigger looked into his son's eyes. "It's over, go on and go. It's over."

TJ hated to leave but he obeyed his father and told Alex to pull off. Truth looked out the window at her father. She cried even harder because she felt like she was losing two parents at one time.

Trigger sat holding Legacy's hands as he heard the sirens coming up the hill. "I'm sorry Cy, Cy, I am so sorry. I failed you. I failed Truth, but I kept my promise and I brought her home."

Several uniformed officers jumped out of the car with their guns drawn. Shouting at him they yelled, "Put your hands in the air and don't move!"

Trigger just sat there holding on to Legacy's hand.

"Put your hands up now!" the officer shouted again.

The entire area was surrounded as more officers pulled up in their squad cars. Trigger looked around at all of the guns drawn at him. Lying next to Legacy was the 357 Magnum she used to kill Assault. One of the officers caught Trigger's eyes on the gun and moved in closer.

"Don't you fucking move. Get your hands up in the air right now Dammit!" The officer was hoping he did not have to kill yet another black man who wanted to commit suicide by way of police.

Trigger contemplated going for the gun knowing he would be pumped full of lead if he did. The officer moved on him just in time before he was able to grab it and threw his face into the gravel.

"You are under arrest, anything you say can and will be held against you...."

Trigger tuned out the officer reading his Miranda rights as he was pulled to his feet. He watched as they placed Legacy's body on a gurney and put her into an ambulance.

He was numb to everything around him including the excessive force the police used when they shoved him in the back of the squad car. He dropped his head down and wished he were the one on the gurney. The squad car drove away to take Trigger to his new home, behind bars.

CHAPTER TWELVE

A FINAL GOODBYE!

She drive to the city was quiet. TJ and Taz were worried about Truth. She had stopped crying and was staring out the window of the truck. They had already mutually decided that she could stay with one of them.

Truth's heart was broken. Never had she felt pain such as she had felt that day. She didn't know if she could continue in life without her mother. She sat staring out the window reminiscing about the arguments and all the times her mother tried to instill words of wisdom to her about men and sex. Truth thought about the time when she was twelve and wanted to wear a mini skirt to school. Legacy had snatched the skirt right off of her and burned it. Smiling Truth laughed causing both of her brothers to turn and look at her strangely. They thought she was going crazy. Arriving back at Truth's house no one said anything. They knew that they would eventually have to relocate. The murder of Assault and T-money would cause retaliation from their people which would be too much for them to handle alone. With Trigger in police custody their resources were limited.

Sitting on the porch was a young man around Truth's age.

He was pacing the stairs when he saw them drive up. TJ had his hand on his gun as he jumped out.

"Who the hell are you?" he asked him.

The young man looked at TJ and saw his hand on his gun. His eyes grew wide and he was nervous all over again. "I don't want any trouble at all. I was just looking for the woman of this house."

TJ looked him over. He was a square type nigga with a button up Polo shirt and khaki pants. He looked like a college student. Truth stepped out of the truck curious to know who he was.

"Get back in the truck Truth. I'll handle this." TJ said. He was still unsure of the guy's business and didn't want to take a chance in case it was a set up.

She didn't listen and approached anyway.

"You must be Truth." The young man said.

"How do you know my name and what are you doing here?" Truth was staring at him.

"It's a long story but is your mother here?"

Truth dropped her head. Fresh tears started to form in her eyes.

TJ didn't like seeing Truth cry so he was going to do his best to make the young man leave. "Look, now is not a good time. I don't know who you are and what business you have here but you need to leave."

"I know this may sound weird but, well, let me introduce myself first. My name is Tevin Marshall. I....well almost 19 years ago I was adopted."

"And what? Is this the house you grew up in? I mean if you trying to do a story and reminisce and shit now ain't the fucking time." TJ was done hearing him talk.

Tevin just stared at him and frowned. "Legacy Marshall

lives here and she is my mother." He said relieved to have gotten it out.

Truth looked up at him and frowned.

"How the fuck Legacy yo' mother? She only had one child and she is standing right here?" TJ pointed at Truth.

Taz who was sitting in the truck rolled down the window after watching the three of them on the porch. His knee was still in pain from his gunshot wound and he wanted to get to a doctor.

"Damn man, who the hell is that and why ya'll taking so long, we need to go fo' the cops be all over this mutha fucka."

Truth had a million questions to ask Tevin. Her mother never said, anything about any other kids so she knew he had to be lying.

"My mother never had any other kids but me. I am her only child. She had me when she was 15 years old." Truth said

Pulling out a piece of paper Tevin showed her his adoption papers. "She gave me up when she was 13 because she was too young to care for a baby. I have everything right here showing where her parents made her sign. My father was her step brother and I learned later she was raped by him and had me."

Truth and TJ's mouths dropped open.

Shaking her head Truth could not understand why her mother kept it a secret all these years.

"I don't mean to ask a lot of questions but why did you cry when I asked if she was here?"

Looking at him Truth was angry. "Because she's dead! My momma is dead. If you are looking to get rich or whatever the fuck you are on you can forget it. I will fight you until I am in my own grave before you get anything from my mother.!" Truth was shaking.

TJ pulled her in his arms as she sobbed.

"Look you uppity ass muthafucka it's time for you to roll. My sister been through enough bullshit for today."

Tevin was not satisfied. He wanted to know what happened. He searched too long for Legacy to just take the fact she was dead. He remembered seeing her at the hospital when Truth had been shot. He wanted to approach her then but was scared she would reject him. He remembered her face and her eyes. They were comforting to him and he had to see her again. He grabbed his bag and his papers and walked off the porch. Turning around he looked at Truth who was holding on to TJ. "I'm sorry to hear about your mother," he dropped his head and turned around to leave.

Truth stood up. "Look Tevin, it's not your fault ok. It's just been a long day. I'll give you my number and you can call me in a few weeks and I'll tell you what you want to know," she wiped her eyes with her hand "Thanks, I'd like that," he walked to his car and got in driving off.

At the Precinct

• • •

"Tavarius Morrow, do you know what you are up against here? You could be charged with the murder of Aquarius "Assault" Garvey, Terry "T-money" Mitchell, Jason Averex, Kendrick Watson, Damon Washington, Timothy Edwards. I could go on and on for all the bodies found including Legacy Marshall."

Sitting in the room Trigger had remained silent until they mentioned Legacy's name. "I didn't kill Legacy Marshall muthafucka ."

The officer circled the table and looked at him. Taking a puff from his cigarette he wanted to make Trigger give up any information but he wasn't talking. Grabbing a folder he slammed several pictures that were taken at the scene of all of the bodies including Legacy's. Trigger skipped over all of the pictures but couldn't help looking at Legacy's picture. Her face was soft and she looked asleep. The blood on her chest made him nauseous. His Legacy was really gone.

"Did you hear what I said? You are gonna face life in prison without parole when this goes before a grand jury." The officer yelled at him.

"Where is my fucking lawyer."

"Even if you had Johnnie Cochran you couldn't get a out of this. You know how long we've been wanting to get your ass off the streets? DO YOU?" He got down in Trigger's face.

Another officer walked in followed by two other detectives.

"What you got?" The officer with the Sherman Hemsley hair style asked.

Pulling him to the side he whispered to the other officer, "Honestly, not a damn thing as usual, his fingerprints are on nothing. He could go for self defense here and end up right back on the streets."

Frowning the detective looked over Trigger's record. "Mr. Morrow. I see we meet again. With all of what you have been through I would think that you would get sick of seeing my face." He leaned down staring Trigger in the eyes. "I believe you won't be seeing the light of day again."

"Man fuck you, where is my lawyer," Trigger asked again getting agitated at all of them.

"I am right here." His lawyer Michael Graham said as he came through the door.

He was a tall and very muscular gentlemen. He sat down next to Trigger.

"Excuse me gentlemen, if I can have a moment with my client here."

They all looked at him.

The officers agreed to leave the room, they grabbed all the pictures of all and exited the room. Trigger sat back in his chair and stared at the ceiling.

"Tavarius, I have to warn you this is a case even I may not be able to beat."

"How much is it gonna take?"

"It's not even about money right now. Do you know they are trying to charge you for two murders that happened about 8 months ago?"

Trigger thought for a second. He had killed so many people he never remembered who they were. "And who are they?" He asked.

"Some young guy named Cameron "Cabbie" Jackson. They are trying to charge you because his brother came forward and told them he saw you shoot him when really it was his friend who saw the murder but he won't tell. You bailed out for the one for Thomas Maple but the family wants to go on with the proceedings. Your trial date for that one is scheduled in two weeks." His lawyer stopped talking and looked at him.

Trigger was nonchalant. He didn't really care about either one of the men that were mentioned.

Leaning forward he looked Trigger in the eyes. "Man, I was sorry to hear about Legacy and if I were in your shoes I would have done the same thing to protect my daughter."

Trigger looked back at him. "You know, I knew when that girl was born I was going to go to jail for her. I just knew it. I'm not sorry for anything and if you want to put that on record do so."

Trigger folded his hands.

"Well what I can do for you is get you out of here for Legacy's funeral if you want to go. Of course you'll be in handcuffs and there will be security there."

"I wouldn't have it any other way."

They shook hands and the attorney exited the room.

• • •

Somewhere on the East Side

"Man you know the plan so stick to it. No bullshitting and we can get it done." Some guy was smoking a cigarette and pacing the floor. Three of them were standing around listening to the one speaking.

"How the hell we gon' do it? Security gon' be tight in that bitch."

"Don't worry about that, I got connections. Just make sure ya'll there on time, not even one minute late or everything can be fucked up." Dude grabbed the bottle of Remy and poured the liquor into several shot glasses. Passing them around he raised his in the air. "Fo' ma niggas who ain't here, and in the name of my little brother, Cabbie. We gon' do this fo you baby."

They all clinked glasses and downed the shots.

• • •

Sitting at the funeral home in the front row wearing all black, Truth tried to hold it together. Just the week before she had attended the funeral of her best friend, Taysha. Now she was sitting front row staring at her mother's lifeless body. Her Aunt Tessa was crying and rocking being held by her husband and her other sister. TJ and Taz had agreed to attend the funeral to be Truth's support and were sitting on either sides of her. Truth watched as the people got up one by one to view the body before the actual service began. She saw Tevin approach the casket.

"What the fuck is that nigga doing here?" TJ whispered to her.

Shrugging her shoulders Truth kept her eye on him. She found it funny that he actually shed a tear for a woman he barely even knew. Truth wanted to tell him about her mother's drug and alcohol addiction and the incident in New York. Deciding it was best to let his memory of her go untainted she told him all the good things. He placed red roses inside of Legacy's casket between her closed hands and sat down. There was a verbal commotion at the back of the church when police officers escorted Trigger in. He was wearing a black suit and was handcuffed with his hands in front of him. Truth, TJ and Taz all turned to see him.

"At least they let him wear a suit and didn't make him come in one of those hideous jail suits." Taz said to TJ who nodded his head in agreement.

Truth's eyes locked with her father's as he walked down the aisle towards the casket.

He winked his eye at her and mouthed the words *I love you* to her. He nodded his head at his sons who nodded back. He was proud of them for sticking by their sister in her time of need and knew she would be ok as long as they had her back. Looking down in the casket he looked at Legacy's still body. Her face was ashen in color and her features were soft. She was wearing a dress he had bought her when she had come home from the hospital after giving birth to Truth 18 years ago. It cost him $700 for the dress and it was navy blue. She loved the dress because it was the first expensive item besides tennis shoes or jeans that he had bought her. Trigger had got it for her when she left her bag at home. He remembered how elated she was. She had told him, *"Oh my God, this thing had to cost some money. If I ever was to die I would want to be buried in it*

177

so that no one else could wear it."

Trigger smiled slightly thinking Legacy must have told Truth about it. He tried not to shed a tear but he missed Legacy terribly and regretted all of the times they fought about Truth.

Truth started crying again when she saw a tear slip from her father's eyes. She got up out of her seat and approached him at the casket. She slipped her arms around him and hugged him. He looked at his baby girl and broke down almost losing his balance. The officers had to help hold him up. There wasn't a dry eye in the house even TJ and Taz were wiping their eyes.

"Truth...." He whispered, "Always remember no one is stronger than you but GOD. Never fear any man, no matter what and remember you are *my* BABY GIRL, you are the TRUTH. No one and nothing will ever change that."

Truth nodded her head as the tears continued to fall. She leaned forward so he could kiss her forehead. She hugged him again before they were urged to take their seats so the service could begin. After the preacher's eulogy, guiding Legacy right into heaven saying all sinners would be forgiven, it was time to put her casket into the herse waiting outside. The pallbearers took their place beside the casket. TJ and Taz noticed something strange about two of the pallbearers who kept looking at Trigger. As they picked up the casket the four men carried it down the church aisle with Truth directly behind it and Trigger, escorted by the police, behind her. TJ and Taz stood directly behind the officers. As they pushed the casket into the back of the vehicle TJ caught eye contact with one of the pallbearers who had on dark sun glasses. In the blink of an eye the other pallbearer pulled out a pistol from his waistband and yelled out, "In the name of Cabbie, muthafucka," and fired off his gun.

TJ yelled noticing Truth was in the line of fire and pushed

her out of the way. The officers tried to push Trigger out of the way and pulled their weapons to fire back, but Trigger was unmoving. He stood still as the culprits pumped bullets into his chest. He fell to his knees. He was still alive but bleeding profusely. He knew he would not survive that incident. He looked up at the sky as the pain and burning became unbearable. With tears in his eyes he felt the breeze across his cheek. He could hear his mother in his head telling him a change is gonna come. *Lord please take me now and watch over my children, let them be more than me. Mom and Dad, I am coming to join you. Legacy and Tasty, I pray you two can forgive me when I get there. Save a spot for me.* He silently prayed before he died.

The front of the church was total chaos. People were screaming and crying. TJ and Taz were on their knees next to Trigger's body willing him to come back. Surprisingly Truth stood still, not even a tear had dropped from her face. She had a dream the night before that her father was going to be killed. She knew it was only a matter of time because he had escaped death too many times. She placed her hand on the casket and closed her eyes. She heard her father's words in her head *Fear no man but God. You are my Baby Girl.* In one swift move Truth pulled out the small pistol her father had given to her when she was 13. It was small enough to fit into her purse. Just as he had taught his boys to stay strapped he taught his daughter to do the same but figured he would always be around to protect her so she would never have to use it. Normally she didn't carry it but she started making sure it was on her after she had been kidnapped. She saw the two men who shot her father running off towards a car. She aimed and pulled the trigger twice shooting one in the back of the head and the other in the neck. She watched their bodies fall and quickly shoved the gun back into her purse. Due to all of the chaos around her father no one noticed that she had shot anyone except Taz, who had just in time lifted his head to catch sight of her arm and the target she was aiming at. She was calm and extremely collected as she joined her brothers on the steps by their father. The police that were with Trigger had called for an ambulance and back up. Taz had told TJ about what Truth had done and they both were looking at her nodding their heads in approval because they would have done the same thing. Truth watched as her father's body was placed on a gurney and put into an ambulance. She along with her brothers then got into the awaiting limo and went to the gravesite to bury her mother. A week later after an autopsy was performed Tavarius Edwin Morrow a.k.a. "Trigger," was buried beside his lifelong love and the mother of his beloved Baby Girl.

MOVING ON!

After burying her parents and collecting over a million dollars from her fathers' insurance policy, along with all of the money he had stashed in several different spots, Truth decided to move out of Los Angeles. Every block and every street reminded her of her father. She didn't want any memories of that lifestyle. She was able to sell the house she once lived in with her mother to her brother, Tevin, who was going to remodel it and rent it out. She got to know him on a personal level and found that they were a lot alike. She chose Columbus, Ohio to move to when she heard Taz was moving there to be with his son and to marry Ebony.

"Now you know they got some fine ass niggas there girl and even though you grieving now I'm sure you gon' find you one." Kyisha said to Truth the night before on the phone.

Truth just shook her head. She packed up all of her clothes

into the awaiting Uhaul truck.

TJ showed up with his own bags packed. He was moving to the same city along with Shaquena and his son. All three of them had split the money from selling what the police did not confiscate. Because the mansion was in Tasty it was left behind along with the cars that were stored in the garage below. The grand total split between the three children was 500,000.

"I can't believe he's gone. It's sad to say but the city seems quiet." TJ said.

"Yeah it does, I'm sure LAPD is more than overjoyed."

TJ just shook his head.

A red car was creeping around the corner near where the Uhaul truck was parked. TJ stopped talking and looked up. Truth caught him looking at something and turned her attention to the car he was looking at. Afraid it was one of Assault's boys or T-money's crew TJ ducked behind the truck and pulled out his gun. Truth pulled out her .38 and was ready in case there was any drama. Taz pulled up in the red car and rolled down the window. He started laughing. He stared down the barrel of Truth's gun.

"Damn, you can tell you a gangsta's daughter, look at you, you got the gun all cocked and shit, ready to blow my fucking head off."

Truth put the gun away.

"Don't play, you know how I gotta do it."

"Nigga you was about to be another dead relative, whose car is this anyway?" TJ said looking at the red, Dodge Magnum.

"Shit nigga, it's mine, I just picked it up and drove it right off the showroom floor. Is ya'll niggas ready or what, it won't be long for a hit is put out on us. Plus I gotta hurry up and get to Ohio, I got grade A trim waiting on a brother."

Both TJ and Truth turned their nose up.

"Yeah man we ready, Quena is already in Ohio she just told me her plane touched down an hour ago." TJ said.

The three of them piled into Taz's new car after giving the keys to the Uhaul to a driver they hired.

Truth looked at her old house one more time and closed her eyes really hard. She could see her mother standing with her father waving and smiling at her. She waved back as the car pulled off. She opened her eyes long enough to see the truck that was headed straight for them at high speed, but it was too late.

● ● ●

Two weeks later

At her friends' gravesite Kyisha knelt down next to the headstone. On it read, "Rest in Peace Baby Girl, you were always the Truth."

Wiping her face she sighed and stepped over the headstones of Tavarius Jr a.k.a TJ, Tamaz a.k.a. Taz, and Truth "Baby Girl" Morrow all killed by a drunk driver.

Flower's Bed

Most Controversial Book Of This Era

Written By

Antoine "Inch" Thomas

Suspenseful...Fastpaced...Richly Textured

PUBLISHED BY AMIAYA ENTERTAINMENT

From the Underground Bestseller "Flower's Bed"
Author Antoine "Inch" Thomas delivers you

NO REGRETS

It's Time To Get It Popping

"Gritty....Realistic Conflicts....Intensely Eerie"
Published by Amiaya Entertainment

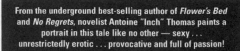

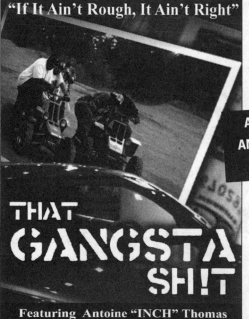

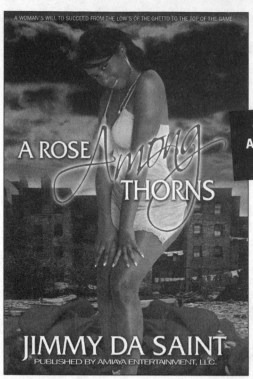

STORIES FROM AND INSPIRED BY THE STREETS

SOCIAL SECURITY

IN THE HOOD WE TAKE CARE OF OUR OWN

PARENTAL ADVISORY EXPLICIT CONTENT

PUBLISHED BY AMIAYA ENTERTAINMENT, LLC.

T. Benson Glover takes you on a journey to the "Badlands".

Phone

Sister

T. BENSON GLOVER

PUBLISHED BY AMIAYA ENTERTAINMENT, LLC.

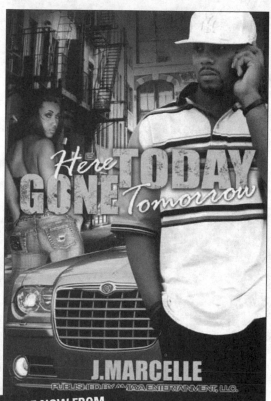

Truth Hurts

ORDER FORM

Number of Copies

Truth Hurts	ISBN# 0-9777544-2-1	$15.00/Copy	_____
Here Today Gone Tomorrow	ISBN# 0-9777544-6-4	$15.00/Copy	_____
Social Security	ISBN# 0-9777544-4-8	$15.00/Copy	_____
Sister	ISBN# 0-9777544-3-X	$15.00/Copy	_____
A Rose Among Thorns	ISBN# 0-9777544-0-5	$15.00/Copy	_____
That Gangsta Sh!t Vol. II	ISBN# 0-9777544-1-3	$15.00/Copy	_____
So Many Tears	ISBN# 0-9745075-9-8	$15.00/Copy	_____
Hoe-Zetta	ISBN# 0-9745075-8-X	$15.00/Copy	_____
All Or Nothing	ISBN# 0-9745075-7-1	$15.00/Copy	_____
Against The Grain	ISBN# 0-9745075-6-3	$15.00/Copy	_____
Ain't Mad At Ya	ISBN# 0-9745075-5-5	$15.00/Copy	_____
Diamonds In The Rough	ISBN# 0-9745075-4-7	$15.00/Copy	_____
Flower's Bed	ISBN# 0-9745075-0-4	$14.95/Copy	_____
That Gangsta Sh!t	ISBN# 0-9745075-3-9	$15.00/Copy	_____
No Regrets	ISBN# 0-9745075-1-2	$15.00/Copy	_____
Unwilling To Suffer	ISBN# 0-9745075-2-0	$15.00/Copy	_____

PRIORITY POSTAGE (4-6 DAYS US MAIL): Add $4.95

Accepted form of Payments: Institutional Checks or Money Orders
(All Postal rates are subject to change.)
Please check with your local Post Office for change of rate and schedules.
Please Provide Us With Your Mailing Information:

Billing Address_____
Name: _____
Address:_____
Suite/Apartment#: _____
City:_____
Zip Code:_____

Shipping Address
Name:_____
Address:_____
Suite/Apartment#:_____
City:_____
Zip Code:_____

(Federal & State Prisoners, Please include your Inmate Registration Number)

Send Checks or Money Orders to:
AMIAYA ENTERTAINMENT
P.O.BOX 1275
NEW YORK, NY 10159
212-946-6565

www.amiayaentertainment.com